William Shakespeare's Troilus and Cressida: A Retelling in Prose

David Bruce

Published by David Bruce, 2022.

This is a work of fiction. Similarities to real people, places, or events are entirely coincidental.

WILLIAM SHAKESPEARE'S TROILUS AND CRESSIDA: A RETELLING IN PROSE

First edition. July 29, 2022.

Copyright © 2022 David Bruce.

ISBN: 979-8201969639

Written by David Bruce.

Table of Contents

Dedication

Dedicated to Carl Eugene Bruce and Josephine Saturday Bruce

My father, Carl Eugene Bruce, died on 24 October 2013. He used to work for Ohio Power, and at one time, his job was to shut off the electricity of people who had not paid their bills. He sometimes would find a home with an impoverished mother and some children. Instead of shutting off their electricity, he would tell the mother that she needed to pay her bill or soon her electricity would be shut off. He would write on a form that no one was home when he stopped by because if no one was home he did not have to shut off their electricity.

The best good deed that anyone ever did for my father occurred after a storm that knocked down many power lines. He and other linemen worked long hours and got wet and cold. Their feet were freezing because water got into their boots and soaked their socks. Fortunately, a kind woman gave my father and the other linemen dry socks to wear.

My mother, Josephine Saturday Bruce, died on 14 June 2003. She used to work at a store that sold clothing. One day, an impoverished mother with a baby clothed in rags walked into the store and started shoplifting in an interesting way: The mother took the rags off her baby and dressed the infant in new clothing. My mother knew that this mother could not afford to buy the clothing, but she helped the mother dress her baby and then she watched as the mother walked out of the store without paying.

***

The doing of good deeds is important. As a free person, you can choose to live your life as a good person or as a bad person. To be a good person, do good deeds. To be a bad person, do bad deeds. If you do good deeds, you will become good. If you do bad deeds, you will become bad. To become the person you want to be, act as if you already are that kind of person. Each of us chooses what kind of person we will become. To become a good person, do the things a good person does. To become a bad person, do the things a bad person does. The opportunity to take action to become the kind of person you want to be is yours.

Human beings have free will. According to the Babylonian Niddah 16b, whenever a baby is to be conceived, the Lailah (angel in charge of contraception) takes the drop of semen that will result in the conception and asks God, "Sovereign of the Universe, what is going to be the fate of this drop? Will it develop into a robust or into a weak person? An intelligent or a stupid person? A wealthy or a poor person?" The Lailah asks all these questions, but it does not ask, "Will it develop into a righteous or a wicked person?" The answer to that question lies in the decisions to be freely made by the human being that is the result of the conception.

A Buddhist monk visiting a class wrote this on the chalkboard: "EVERYONE WANTS TO SAVE THE WORLD, BUT NO ONE WANTS TO HELP MOM DO THE DISHES." The students laughed, but the monk then said, "Statistically, it's highly unlikely that any of you will ever have the opportunity to run into a burning orphanage and rescue an infant. But, in the smallest gesture of kindness — a warm smile, holding the door for the person behind you, shoveling the driveway of the elderly person next door — you have committed an act of immeasurable profundity, because to each of us, our life is our universe."

In her book titled *I Have Chosen to Stay and Fight*, comedian Margaret Cho writes, "I believe that we get complimentary snack-size portions of the afterlife, and we all receive them in a different way." For Ms. Cho, many of her snack-size portions of the afterlife come in hip hop music. Other people get different snack-size portions of the afterlife, and we all must be on the lookout for them when they come our way. And perhaps doing good deeds and experiencing good deeds are snack-size portions of the afterlife.

William Shakespeare's
Troilus and Cressida:
A Retelling in Prose

***

In these retellings, as in all my retellings, I have tried to make the work of literature accessible to modern readers who may lack the knowledge about mythology, religion, and history that the literary work's contemporary audience had.

Do you know a language other than English? If you do, I give you permission to translate this book, copyright your translation, publish or self-publish it, and keep all the royalties for yourself. (Do give me credit, of course, for the original retelling.)

I would like to see my retellings of classic literature used in schools, so I give permission to the country of Finland (and all other countries) to give copies of this book to all students forever. I also give permission to the state of Texas (and all other states) to give copies of this book to all students forever. I also give permission to all teachers to give copies of this book to all students forever.

Teachers need not actually teach my retellings. Teachers are welcome to give students copies of my eBooks as background material. For example, if they are teaching Homer's *Iliad* and *Odyssey*, teachers are welcome to give students copies of my *Virgil's* Aeneid: *A Retelling in Prose* and tell students, "Here's another ancient epic you may want to read in your spare time."

CAST OF CHARACTERS

Male Characters: Trojan

PRIAM, King of Troy.

HECTOR, Priam's oldest Son. Crown Prince of Troy.

TROILUS, Priam's youngest Son. In love with Cressida. "Troilus" has two syllables. In other works of literature, Polydorus is Priam's youngest son.

PARIS, Priam's Son. Kidnapped Helen, wife of Menelaus, King of Sparta, thereby causing the Trojan War.

DEIPHOBUS, Priam's Son.

HELENUS, Priam's Son. A priest.

MARGARELON, a Bastard Son of Priam.

AENEAS & ANTENOR, Trojan Warriors.

CALCHAS, a Trojan Priest, taking part with the Greeks.

PANDARUS, Uncle to Cressida.

Male Characters: Greek

AGAMEMNON, the Greek General.

MENELAUS, his Brother. Menelaus is the lawful husband of Helen, whom Paris, Prince of Troy, ran away with.

ACHILLES, Greek Warrior.

AJAX, Greek Warrior. In this play, Ajax' mother is Hesione, sister to Priam, King of Troy. This makes him the first cousin of Hector, whose father is Priam. In other works of literature, it is Teucer, Ajax' half-brother (they share the same father), whose mother is Hesione.

ULYSSES, Greek Warrior. Ulysses is his Roman name; his Greek name is Odysseus.

NESTOR, Greek Advisor. Nestor is aged.

DIOMEDES, Greek Warrior.

PATROCLUS, Greek Warrior. Friend to Achilles.

THERSITES, a deformed and scurrilous Greek.

ALEXANDER, Servant to Cressida.

Servant to Troilus.

Servant to Paris.

Servant to Diomedes.

Female Characters

HELEN, Legal Wife to Menelaus. Kidnapped by Paris. In many works of literature, it is ambiguous whether Helen went willingly with Paris.

ANDROMACHE, Wife to Hector.

CASSANDRA, Daughter to Priam. She is a prophetess.

CRESSIDA, Daughter to Calchas.

Minor Characters

Trojan and Greek Soldiers, and Attendants.

Note

Ilium, Ilion: These are other names for Troy.

PROLOGUE

"Our scene lies in Troy. From the isles of Greece, proud Princes, their noble blood enraged, to the port of Athens have sent their ships, fraught with the soldiers and weapons of cruel war. Sixty-nine Princes, who wore their regal coronets, from the Athenian bay put forth toward Phrygia, site of Troy, and their vow is made to ransack Troy, within whose strong walls the kidnapped Helen, Menelaus' Queen, sleeps with wanton, lecherous Paris, and that is the reason for the Trojan War.

"To Tenedos, an island near Troy, they come, and the large ships that displace much water disgorge there their warlike fraughtage — their cargo fraught with danger to Trojans. Now on the Dardan — Trojan — plains the fresh and still unbruised Greeks pitch their splendid pavilions. Priam's city has six gates named Dardan, Tymbria, Helias, Chetas, Troien, and Antenorides; they have massive metal brackets and corresponding bolts that fit in the brackets to lock the gates. This city stirs up the sons of Troy. Now expectation that tickles lively spirits on one and the other side, Trojan and Greek, leads them to risk everything — winner take all.

"And hither I have come. I am an armed Prologue telling you all this, but I am not armed with an author's pen or actor's voice, but instead I am suited with armor and am carrying weapons as is relevant to our theme and story. I am here to tell you, fair beholders, that our book leaps over the first battles and their results; instead, our book starts and then ends with what may be recounted as relevant to the theme of this book. This book will not tell you how the war started but will instead begin *in medias res* — in the middle of the war.

"Like this book or find fault with it; do what you please. Whether good or bad, it is but the chance of war."

CHAPTER 1

— 1.1 —

Troilus and Pandarus stood before Priam's palace. Troilus was the youngest son of Priam, King of Troy, and he was in love with Cressida, the niece of Pandarus. The time was morning, and Troilus had put on his armor in preparation to fight the Greeks outside the city of Troy.

"Call here my servant; I'll take off my armor," Troilus said. "Why should I make war outside the walls of Troy, when I find such cruel battle here within myself? Let each Trojan who is master of his heart go to the battlefield. I, Troilus, unfortunately have no heart because I have given it to Cressida."

"Will this problem never be solved?" Pandarus asked.

Troilus said, "The Greeks are strong and skillful in proportion to their strength, they are fierce in proportion to their skill, and they are valiant in proportion to their fierceness, but I am weaker than a woman's tear, tamer than sleep, more foolish than ignorance, less valiant than the virgin in the night, and as without skills as unpracticed and inexperienced infancy."

"Well, I have told you enough of this," Pandarus said. "As for my part, I'll not concern myself any further. He who will have a cake made out of wheat must wait for the wheat to be ground into flour."

"Haven't I waited?"

"Yes, you have waited for the grinding, but you must also wait for the bolting — the sifting — of the flour," Pandarus said.

"Haven't I waited?"

"Yes, you have waited for the bolting, but you must also wait for the leavening. You must wait for the dough to rise."

"I have also waited for that," Troilus said.

"Yes, you have waited for the leavening; but the waiting also includes the kneading, the making of the cake, the heating of the oven and the baking. Indeed, you must wait for the cake to cool, too, or you may chance to burn your lips."

Pandarus was making a series of bawdy puns. "Grinding" referred to the act of sex — grinding crotch against crotch. "Bolt" referred to penis. "Leavening" referred to a developing pregnancy. "Oven" was a slang word for vagina or womb.

"Patience herself, whatever goddess she is, flinches less at suffering than I do," Troilus said. "I suffer greatly from unrequited love. I sit at Priam's royal table, and when beautiful Cressida comes into my thoughts — I am a traitor when I say that because for her to come into my thoughts she would have to be absent from my thoughts, and she is never absent from my thoughts!"

"Last night she looked more beautiful than I have ever seen her — or any other woman — look," Pandarus said.

"I was about to tell you — when my heart, as if a sigh had been wedged into it, would split in two, then lest Hector or my father should perceive that I am in love, I have, as when the Sun comes out and lights up a storm, buried this sigh in the wrinkle of a smile. However, a sorrow that is concealed by the appearance and not the reality of gladness is like a laugh that fate turns to sudden sadness."

"If Cressida's hair were not somewhat darker than Helen's — well, forget I said that — there would be no comparison between the women: Cressida would be regarded as the greater beauty. But, of course, she is my relative, my niece, and so I don't want to praise her because I would be called biased, but I wish that somebody — such as you — had heard her talk yesterday, as I did. I will not dispraise your sister Cassandra's wit, but —"

"Oh, Pandarus!" Troilus said. "I tell you, Pandarus — when I tell you that there my hopes lie drowned, don't tell me how many fathoms deep my hopes are submerged. I tell you that I am mad — insane — because of my love for Cressida, and you tell me that she is beautiful. In doing that, you pour in the open ulcer of my heart her eyes, her hair, her cheek, her gait, and her voice. You handle in your discourse — you talk about her — oh, her hand, in whose comparison all other white hands are as black as ink, writing their own reproach, and compared to the softness of her hand the young swan's down is harsh and the gentlest touch is as hard as the palm of a plowman. When I say I love her, you tell me these things, and these things are true. But by saying such things, you put, instead of medicinal oil and balm, in every gash that unrequited love has given me the knife that made those gashes."

"I speak no more than truth," Pandarus said.

"You do not speak the full truth," Troilus replied. "She is more beautiful than you say she is."

"Indeed, I'll not meddle in this love you have for her. Let her be as she is. If she is fair, it is the better for her; and if she is not fair, she has the remedy in her own hands. She can wear cosmetics."

"Good Pandarus, what are you saying, Pandarus!"

"I have had my labor for my trouble," Pandarus said. "I am ill thought of by her and ill thought of by you. I have gone between you and her, but I have received small thanks for my labor."

"What, are you angry, Pandarus? Are you angry with me?"

"Because Cressida is related to me, I say that she's not as beautiful as Helen, lest I be thought biased in the favor of my niece. But if Cressida were not related to me, I would say that she is as beautiful in her everyday clothing as Helen is in her Sunday best. But what do I care? I don't care if Cressida is black and ugly; it is all one and the same to me whether she is ugly or beautiful."

"Did I say that she is not beautiful?"

"I do not care whether you do or not," Pandarus said. "She's a fool to stay in Troy after her father, Calchas, deserted the Trojans and joined the Greeks. Let her go to the Greeks and join her father; that is what I'll tell her the next time I see her. As for me, I'll meddle no more and do no more in this matter."

"Pandarus —"

"I said I won't, and I won't."

"Sweet Pandarus —"

"Please, speak no more to me. I will leave everything the way I found it, and that's the end to my participation."

As Pandarus exited, military trumpets sounded.

Troilus said to himself, "Be quiet, you ungracious clamors! Be quiet, you rude, cacophonous sounds! Fools on both sides! Helen must necessarily be beautiful, when with your blood you daily paint her thus — your blood is the stuff of her cosmetics. I cannot fight upon this point of contention; why should I fight because of Helen? She is too starved and meager a subject for my sword. She is not a good reason for me to risk my life in battle.

"But Pandarus — gods, how you plague me! I cannot come to Cressida except by Pandarus, and he's as peevish and fretful to be wooed to woo as she is stubbornly chaste against all wooing.

"Tell me, Apollo, you loved Daphne, who fled from you and was metamorphosed into a laurel tree. Tell me, for your love of Daphne, what

Cressida is, what Pandarus is, and what I am. Cressida's bed is analogous to wealthy India; there she lies, a pearl. Let the area between Priam's palace and where she resides be called the wild and wandering ocean. I will be the merchant, and this sailing Pandarus will be my uncertain hope, my convoy, and my ship. I hope to use Pandarus to take me to Cressida, and I hope that I will take possession of her."

Military trumpets sounded once more as Aeneas walked over to Troilus.

"How are you, Prince Troilus? Why aren't you on the battlefield?"

"Because I am not there. This woman's answer — 'because' — is fitting because it is womanish for a man to stay away from the battlefield. Aeneas, what is the news from the battlefield today?"

"Paris is wounded and has returned home."

"Aeneas, who wounded him?"

"Troilus, he was wounded by Menelaus."

"Let Paris bleed; it is but a scar to scorn; Paris is gored with Menelaus' horn."

The wound was a scar to scorn because Paris had scorned Menelaus by running away with Helen, Menelaus' wife, and Paris would bear a scar from the wound that he would not have received had he respected Menelaus. Menelaus had horns to use to wound Paris because Paris had cuckolded him. A cuckold is a man whose wife is unfaithful; in this culture, people joked that cuckolds had horns on their head. The scar could be scorned also because a cuckold gave the wound — and resulting scar — to a cuckold-maker instead of the wound's being received for a worthier reason.

Again, military trumpets sounded.

Aeneas said, "Listen! What good sport is out of the city and on the battlefield today!"

"The sport would be better at home, if 'I wish I might' were 'yes, I may,'" Troilus replied.

"Sport" means entertainment. Aeneas used it to refer to the excitement of fighting in a battle; Troilus used it to refer to the excitement of 'fighting' in a bed in which there was a woman.

Troilus added, "But about the sport on the battleground. Are you going there?"

"Yes, and quickly."

"Come, let us go together."
They exited.

Cressida and Alexander, one of her servants, spoke together on a street in Troy.

"Who were those people who went by just now?" Cressida asked.

"Queen Hecuba and Helen," Alexander answered.

"And where are they going?"

"Up to the eastern tower, whose commanding height makes all the low-lying land its subject. They want to see the battle. Hector, whose patience is normally steadfast like all virtues, today was in a bad mood. He rebuked Andromache and struck his armorer, and, just as if there were husbandry in war, before the Sun rose he put on light armor, and he went to the battlefield, where every flower, as if they were prophets, wept with dew at what they foresaw — many deaths of Greeks — in Hector's wrath."

"What was the cause of Hector's anger?" Cressida asked.

"The rumor is that it was this: There is among the Greeks a lord of Trojan blood who is first cousin to Hector. They call him Ajax."

"I understand, but what of him?"

"They say he is a thoroughgoing man in himself, and stands alone."

"So do all men, unless they are drunk, are sick, or have no legs," Cressida joked.

"Lady, Ajax has robbed many beasts of their particular distinctions," Alexander said. "He is as valiant as the lion, as churlish as the bear, and as slow as the elephant. He is a man into whom nature has so crowded moods and dispositions that his valor is crushed into folly and his folly is sauced with discretion: His courage is definitely mixed with folly, and his folly is seasoned with discretion — what is good in him is mixed with what is bad, and what is bad in him has a touch of good. No man has a virtue that Ajax has not a glimpse of, and no man has a flaw that Ajax has not some stain of it: He is melancholy without cause, and he is merry when he ought not to be merry. He has the joints of everything, but everything is out of joint. He has good qualities as well as bad, and everything is so badly put together that he cannot make good use of his good qualities. He is like Briareus, the mythological monster who has a hundred hands, but he is like a Briareus who has the gout — he has a hundred hands but cannot use them. Or he is like an Argus, a mythological monster who has a hundred eyes, but he is like an Argus who is blind — he has a hundred eyes but cannot use them."

"But how could this man named Ajax, the description of whom makes me smile, make Hector angry?"

"They say that yesterday he fought Hector in the battle and struck him down, the disdain and shame of which has ever since kept Hector fasting and waking. Hector is so angry that he cannot eat or sleep."

Cressida saw someone approaching and asked, "Who is coming here?"

"Madam, it is your uncle Pandarus," Alexander replied.

Cressida said, "Hector's a gallant man."

"As gallant as may be in the world, lady," Alexander said.

As Pandarus joined them, he said, "What's that? What's that?"

"Good morning, uncle Pandarus," Cressida said.

"Good morning, niece Cressida. What are you talking about? Good morning, Alexander. How are you, niece? When were you last at Priam's palace?"

"This morning, uncle," Cressida replied.

"What were you talking about when I came here just now?" Pandarus asked. "Was Hector armed and gone before you came to Priam's palace? Helen was not up, was she?"

"Hector was gone, but Helen was not up."

"I see. Hector was up and stirring early."

"That is what we were talking about, and about Hector's anger."

"Was he angry?" Pandarus asked.

"That is what Alexander here said," Cressida replied.

"True, Hector was angry," Pandarus said. "I know the cause, too. He'll lay about him with his sword today, I can tell them that. He will fight well, and Troilus will not come far behind him. Let the Greeks take heed of Troilus, I can tell them that, too."

"What, is he angry, too?"

"Who, Troilus? Troilus is the better man of the two," Pandarus said.

Pandarus was praising Troilus in an attempt to persuade Cressida to fall in love with him, but Hector was definitely the best Trojan warrior.

"Oh, Jupiter! There's no comparison between the two men," Cressida said.

"What, no comparison between Troilus and Hector? Do you know a man if you see him?"

"Yes, if I ever saw him before and knew him," Cressida said.

"Well, I say Troilus is Troilus," Pandarus said.

"Then you say what I say; for, I am sure that he is not Hector."

"No, he is not, and Hector is not Troilus in some ways."

"That is just and fitting to each of them; each man is himself."

"Himself!" Pandarus said. "You think that Troilus is himself? Alas, poor Troilus! I wish that he were himself."

Pandarus meant that Troilus was not himself because he was suffering from his unrequited love for Cressida.

"So he is," Cressida said. "He is himself."

"That statement is as true as the statement that I walked barefoot to India."

"Troilus is not Hector."

"But is Troilus himself? No, he's not himself. I wish that he were himself! Well, the gods are above; time must befriend him or end him. Well, Troilus, well. I wish that my heart were in her body. No, Hector is not a better man than Troilus."

"Excuse me. I don't believe you."

"He is elder."

In fact, Hector was the eldest son of Priam.

"Pardon me, pardon me," Cressida said. "If you mean that Troilus is elder than Hector, you are wrong."

"The other one — Troilus — has not fully come to maturity," Pandarus said. "You shall tell me another tale about who is the elder and the more mature when the other one — Troilus — has fully come to maturity. Hector shall not have Troilus' intelligence this year. Troilus will be more intelligent than Hector."

"Hector shall not need Troilus' intelligence, if he has his own," Cressida said.

"Nor will Hector have Troilus' qualities."

"No matter."

"Nor his beauty."

"Troilus' beauty would not be becoming for Hector; his own beauty is better."

"You have no judgment, niece," Pandarus said. "Helen herself swore the other day, that Troilus, for a brown complexion — for so it is, I must confess — well, no, his complexion is not brown —"

In this culture, fair complexions were valued more highly than black or suntanned or sunburnt complexions.

"No, it is brown," Cressida said.

"Indeed, to say the truth, his complexion is brown and not brown."

"To say the truth, what you have said is true and not true."

"She praised his complexion above the complexion of Paris."

"Why, Paris has color enough," Cressida said.

"So he has."

"Then Troilus has too much color. If Helen praised his complexion above that of Paris, then his complexion is higher than Paris'. If Paris has color enough, and Troilus has a higher color, then Helen made too flaming — too extravagant — praise for a good complexion. I would like just as much that Helen's golden tongue had praised Troilus for having a copper nose."

A copper nose can be a suntanned nose, but in this culture people who had lost their nose as a result of venereal disease or fighting sometimes wore a prosthetic nose made of copper.

"I swear to you that I think Helen loves Troilus better than Paris," Pandarus said.

"Then she's a merry Greek indeed."

Helen, of course, was Greek, and in this culture a "merry Greek" was a wanton person.

"I am sure she loves Troilus more than she loves Paris," Pandarus said. "She came to him the other day by the bay window — and, you know, he has not more than three or four hairs on his chin —"

"Indeed, a tapster's arithmetic may soon bring his particular hairs to a total," Cressida said.

A tapster is a bartender or a server in a bar. They use arithmetic to total the tabs in the bar.

"Why, he is very young, and yet he is able to lift as much weight, within three pounds, as his brother Hector."

"Is he so young a man and so old a lifter?"

Cressida was punning. A "lifter" is a thief, as in shoplifter.

"But I can prove to you that Helen loves Troilus," Pandarus said. "She came and put her white hand up to his cloven chin —"

Pandarus meant that Troilus had a cleft chin but Cressida pretended that he had said that Troilus' chin was split in two.

"May Juno, Queen of the gods, have mercy!" Cressida said. "How came his chin to be cloven?"

"Why, you know it is dimpled," Pandarus said. "I think his smiling becomes him better than any man in all Phrygia."

"Oh, he smiles valiantly."

"Doesn't he?"

"Oh, yes, as if it were a cloud in autumn."

Cressida was being sarcastic about and critical of Troilus' smile. A sunny day in autumn is often beautiful; a cloudy day in autumn is often dull and dreary. A valiant smile likened to a cloud in autumn could be a reference to the Sun valiantly attempting to shine through the clouds during the season of autumn.

"Why, bah, then, but to prove to you that Helen loves Troilus —"

"Troilus will stand to the proof, if you'll prove it so," Cressida said.

One meaning of what Cressida had said was that Troilus would pass the test if he were tested, but there was a second meaning. She was being bawdy. "To stand" means "to have an erection." She was saying that Troilus would have an erection if Pandarus could prove that Helen loved Troilus.

"Troilus!" Pandarus said. "Why, he esteems Helen no more than I esteem an addled — a rotten — egg."

"If you love an addled egg as well as you love an idle and empty head, you would eat chickens in the shell," Cressida said.

Addled eggs often had an embryonic, but dead, chick inside.

"I cannot choose but laugh, when I think how Helen tickled Troilus' chin," Pandarus said. "Indeed, she has a marvelously white hand, I must necessarily confess —"

"That is a confession you have made without first having been tortured on the rack."

"And Helen spied a white hair on his chin."

"Alas, poor chin!" Cressida said. "Many a wart is richer because it has more hairs than one."

"But there was such laughing! Queen Hecuba laughed so much that her eyes ran over."

"With millstones, but not with tears," Cressida said. She did not understand how this anecdote could be so funny that it would make anyone cry with laughter.

"And Cassandra laughed," Pandarus said.

"But there was more temperate fire under the cooking pot of her eyes," Cressida said. "Did her eyes run over, too?"

Cassandra was not the type of person to laugh much. In mythology, she had the gift of prophecy, but she also had the curse of her prophecies never being believed. And as a prophetess, she knew before other people bad events that would soon occur.

"And Hector laughed."

"At what was all this laughing?" Cressida asked. "What were they laughing at?"

"Indeed, at the white hair that Helen spied on Troilus' chin."

"If it had been a green hair, I would have laughed, too," Cressida said.

"They laughed not so much at the hair as at his ingenious answer."

"What was his answer?"

"Helen said, 'Here's only two and fifty hairs on your chin, and one of them is white.'"

"This is her observation, not his answer," Cressida pointed out.

"That's true; make no question of that," Pandarus replied. "'Two and fifty hairs,' Troilus replied, 'and one hair is white. That white hair is my father, and all the rest are his sons.'"

Troilus was punning. Most of his hairs were heirs — Priam's fifty sons.

Pandarus continued, "'By Jupiter!' said Helen, 'which of these hairs is Paris, my husband?' 'The forked one,' said he. 'Pluck it out, and give it to him.' But there was such laughing! And Helen so blushed, and Paris so fretted, and all the rest so laughed, that it surpasses description."

Priam had fifty sons. Troilus had one white hair, and fifty black hairs, but one black hair was forked (had a split end) and so was counted as two, making a total (in the anecdote) of fifty-two hairs.

The forked hair represented Paris, and the fork in the hair represented horns. Paris had made a cuckold of Menelaus and given him horns, and Troilus was joking that Helen had made a cuckold of Paris and given him horns.

"So let your anecdote pass by now; for it has been a while going by," Cressida said.

"Well, niece," Pandarus said. "I told you something important yesterday; think about it."

The "something important" was Troilus' love for her.

"So I do."

"I'll be sworn it is true; he will weep, as if he were a man born in April, the month of showers."

"And I'll spring up in his tears, as if I were a nettle anticipating May," Cressida said.

She had changed the proverb "April showers bring May flowers" so that she could criticize Troilus.

Trumpets sounded retreat. Now the Trojan warriors would return to Troy.

"Listen," Pandarus said. "The warriors are coming from the battlefield. Shall we stand up here, and see them as they pass toward Troy? Good niece, do, sweet niece Cressida."

"As you wish."

"Here, here, here's an excellent place," Pandarus said. "Here we may see them very well. I'll tell you all their names as they pass by; but be sure to pay special attention to Troilus more than the rest."

"Don't speak so loudly," Cressida said, embarrassed lest Pandarus be overheard.

Aeneas walked by them.

"That's Aeneas," Pandarus said. "Isn't he a splendid man? He's one of the flowers of Troy, I can tell you, but be sure to look at Troilus; you shall see him soon."

Antenor walked by them.

"Who's that?" Cressida asked.

"That's Antenor," Pandarus replied. "He has a shrewd intelligence, I can tell you, and he's a good enough man. He's one of the soundest judges in Troy and has the greatest wisdom, and he is handsome. But when is Troilus coming? I'll show you Troilus soon. If he sees me, you shall see him nod at me."

"Will he give you the nod?"

"Give you the nod" was slang for "make a fool out of you."

"Yes, you will see him nod at me," Pandarus said.

"If he nods at you, the rich shall have more," Cressida said.

Cressida was willing to be critical of Pandarus, her uncle, as well as of Troilus. A noddy is a fool. Cressida was referring to Matthew 13:12, part of which states, *"For whosoever hath, to him shall be given, and he shall have abundance [...]."* If Troilus were to nod to Pandarus, he would make Pandarus a noddee, and Pandarus would be more of a fool than he already was.

Hector walked by them.

"That's Hector, that, that, look, that man," Pandarus said. "There's a fellow!"

He yelled, "Way to go, Hector!"

Then he said to Cressida, "There's a brave man, niece. Oh, brave Hector! Look how he looks! There's a countenance! Isn't he a splendid man?"

"Yes, he is a splendid man!"

"Isn't he, though!" Pandarus said. "Seeing him does a man's heart good. Look at the dents on his helmet! Look yonder, do you see them? Look there. There's no jesting; there's evidence that Hector has been fighting hard in battle and laying blows on the enemy. That's evidence that no naysayers can deny — there are dents in his helmet!"

"Were those dents made by swords?"

"Swords! Yes, and by other weapons such as spears. Hector does not care what enemy he faces. If the Devil were to come to fight him, it's all one to Hector — he doesn't care whether he fights a Greek or the Devil. By God, it does one's heart good to see Hector. But look. Yonder comes Paris, yonder comes Paris."

Paris walked by them.

"Look yonder, niece. Isn't he a gallant man, too, isn't he? Why, this is splendid now. Who said that Paris was wounded and had returned home today? He's not wounded. Why, this will do Helen's heart good now, ha! I wish I could see Troilus now! You shall see Troilus soon."

Helenus walked by them.

"Who's that?" Cressida asked.

"That's Helenus. I wonder where Troilus is. That's Helenus. I think that Troilus did not go out to fight today. That's Helenus."

"Can Helenus fight, uncle?" Cressida asked, aware that Helenus was a priest.

"Helenus? No," Pandarus said. Quickly, he changed his answer — one ought not to criticize a Prince. "Yes, he'll fight moderately well. I wonder where Troilus is. Listen! Don't you hear the people cry 'Troilus'? Helenus is a priest."

"What sneaking fellow comes yonder?" Cressida asked. She knew who the "sneaking fellow" was.

Troilus walked by them.

"Where? Yonder? That's Deiphobus," Pandarus said. He was wrong, but he quickly recognized his mistake and said, "It is Troilus! There's a man, niece!"

He called loudly, "Ha! Brave Troilus! The Prince of chivalry!"

"Be quiet!" Cressida said. "You are embarrassing me, and you yourself ought to be embarrassed. Be quiet!"

"Look at him. Look closely at him," Pandarus said. "Oh, brave Troilus! Look well upon him, niece. Look how his sword is bloodied, and how his helmet is more hacked than Hector's, and see how he looks, and how he walks! Oh, admirable youth! He is not yet twenty-three years old. Keep it up, Troilus, keep it up! If I had a sister who was one of the goddesses known as the Graces, and if I had a daughter who was also a goddess, I would give Troilus his choice of which of them to marry. Oh, admirable man! Paris? Paris is dirt compared to him; and, I promise you that Helen would give one of her eyes to exchange Paris for Troilus."

"Here come more soldiers," Cressida said.

More soldiers walked by them.

"These are asses, fools, dolts!" Pandarus said. "They are chaff and bran, chaff and bran! They are mere porridge after one has eaten meat! We have seen the best men and the best man — Troilus. I could live and die in the eyes of Troilus. Don't look at them! Don't look at them! The eagles are gone. What we see now are crows and jackdaws, crows and jackdaws! I would rather be a man such as Troilus than Agamemnon and all the Greek warriors."

"Among the Greeks is Achilles, who is a better man than Troilus," Cressida said.

"Achilles!" Pandarus said. "He is a cart-driver, a porter, a camel — he is a stupid beast of burden!"

"Well, well," Cressida said.

"'Well, well!'" Pandarus repeated. "Why, don't you have any ability to distinguish a real man among 'men'? Haven't you any eyes? Don't you know what a man is? Aren't birth, beauty, good shape, good conversation, manliness, learning, nobleness, virtue, youth, generosity, and other such things the spice and salt that season a man?"

"Yes, a minced man," Cressida said. "And then they are baked with no date in the pie, for then the man's date's out."

Cressida was criticizing Troilus again. Pandarus had highly praised him and mentioned many good qualities that he claimed that Troilus possessed, but she was questioning his manhood. A date is a phallic-shaped fruit, and she was saying that Troilus' date was staying out of the vaginal pie. One meaning of "to mince" is "to walk very primly," and a stereotype of gay men is that they mince. Another meaning of "mince" is "to cut into very small pieces for cooking." Of course, a man whose date is out is a man who is out of fashion and of lesser value — he is after his sell-by date.

"What a woman you are!" Pandarus said. Aware that she was metaphorically fencing with words against his attempts at persuading her to love Troilus, he said, "One does not know at what ward you lie."

A ward is a parrying — defensive — movement in fencing.

Cressida said, "I lie upon my back, to defend my belly."

To lie on her back to defend her belly — say, against a sexual "attack" — seems to be a poor defensive position for such a purpose. But perhaps she meant that she would rely on her back to defend her belly. Or perhaps she was not much interested in defending her belly if it were "attacked" by the right man.

She added, "I rely upon my wit, to defend my wiles; upon my secrecy, to defend my chastity; upon my mask, to defend my beauty; and upon you, to defend all these."

She could satisfy her wiles — cunningly get her wishes — and then use her wit and intelligence to defend them and keep away from herself any bad consequences. One way for her to defend her reputation for chastity was by keeping silent — not telling anyone about an affair, if she should have one. Like other ladies of the time, she wore a mask when in the Sun to protect her face from being tanned by the Sun. The mask hid her face from the Sun the way her secrecy could hide an affair from being known by other people. She also relied on her uncle to protect her; her father was not present in Troy, and so Pandarus was her male protector in Troy. As her uncle, he had a moral obligation to protect her. However, she may have been sarcastic when she said that she would rely upon him. Events would show that Pandarus was in favor of his niece having an affair with Troilus.

She added, "And at all these wards I lie, at a thousand watches — I will have all these defenses during a thousand sleepless nights."

Cressida was hinting at bawdiness. A thousand nights would be sleepless because a male lover would keep her awake. Because she would not be legally married to the male lover, she would have to rely on her own intelligence and secrecy — and her uncle — to keep other people from learning about the affair.

"Tell me about one of your watches — one of your sleepless nights," Pandarus said.

"No, I'll watch you if I have any sleepless nights, and you are one of the chief things that I will have to carefully watch," Cressida said. "If I cannot ward — defend — what I would not have hit, I can watch you for telling how I took the blow. In other words, if I cannot ward off and keep a penis from penetrating me, I will carefully watch you to guard against your telling on me. Of course, if I get pregnant and my belly swells up and cannot be hidden, then it's past watching. I won't then be able to guard against my sexual activity being known."

In her answer, Cressida was punning on the words "watch" and "ward," aka "defend," which were the duties of a watchman.

"What a woman you are!" Pandarus said.

Troilus' servant, a boy, walked over to them and said to Pandarus, "Sir, my lord wants to speak with you right away."

"Where?" Pandarus asked.

"At your own house; he is taking off his armor there."

"Good boy, tell him I am coming," Pandarus said.

The boy exited.

"I doubt that Troilus is wounded," Pandarus said. "Fare you well, good niece."

"*Adieu,* uncle."

"I'll be with you, niece, by and by."

"To bring me something, uncle?"

"Yes, a token from Troilus."

As Pandarus exited, Cressida said to herself, "By the same token, you are a bawd, a pimp, a procurer."

She paused and then added to herself, "Words, vows, gifts, tears, and love's full sacrifice, he — Pandarus — offers in another's — Troilus' — enterprise, but I see a thousand-fold more in Troilus than there is in the mirror of Pandarus' praise. Yet I hold Troilus off. Women are thought to be Angels while they are being wooed; they are not thought to be worth so much after they are won. Things won are done; joy's soul lies in the doing. A woman who is beloved knows nothing unless she knows this: Men prize the thing they have not gained more than it is worth. No woman has ever known a man to love her as sweetly after he got her than while he was pursuing her. Therefore I teach this maxim out of love: What is achieved is commanded; what is not yet gained is beseeched. When a man has won a woman, he commands her; while he is still pursuing her, he beseeches her. Therefore, although my heart bears much love for Troilus, nothing of my love for him shall in my eyes appear. I love Troilus, but I will not let him know that."

Agamemnon, the elderly advisor Nestor, Ulysses, Menelaus, Diomedes, and other important Greeks met in front of Agamemnon's tent in the Greek camp.

Agamemnon said to the others, "What grief has made your cheeks jaundiced? The ample promise of success that hope makes in all plans begun on Earth below fails at first. We do not immediately receive the promised largeness: Obstacles and disasters grow in the veins of the highest reared plans. These obstacles and disasters are like knots that block the sap and so infect the sound pine and divert its grain, twisting and turning it from its natural course of growth.

"Princes, it is not news to us that we have come so far short of our hope that after seven years of siege Troy's walls still stand. Every planned action of which we have historical record had a period of testing in which the people faced problems that thwarted and did not help them achieve their goal, and that thwarted and did not help them carry out the plan that their abstract thought had formed.

"Why then, you Princes, do you with abashed cheeks look at our deeds, and call them shameful? The troubles we face are indeed nothing other than the protracted trials that great Jove has given to us because the King of gods wants to find persistent constancy in men."

Jove was another name for Jupiter, King of the gods.

Agamemnon continued, "The fineness of men's metal — and mettle — is not found in the favor of Lady Fortune; for then the bold and the cowardly, the wise and the foolish, the well-educated and the unread, and the hard and the soft would all seem to be related to each other and much the same, but it is found instead in the wind and tempest of the frown of Lady Distinction, who with a broad and powerful fan blows air at all, winnowing the light stuff away, and leaving behind whatever has mass or matter — the stuff that by itself lies rich in virtue and unmingled with anything base."

Nestor said, "With due observance of your godlike power, Great Agamemnon, Nestor shall explicate your most recent words. In the reproof of chance lies the true proof of men. To know whether a man is really a man, that man must be tested. When the sea is smooth, many shallow baubles — toy-like boats — dare to sail upon her patient breast, making their way with those ships of nobler bulk! But let the ruffian Boreas — the north wind — once enrage the home of the gentle sea-goddess Thetis, and immediately you see the ships with strong ribs cut through liquid mountains, bounding between the two moist elements — the sea and the air — like the hero Perseus' winged horse, Pegasus. Where then is the saucy, insolent boat whose weak sides lack a strong frame? A moment ago, such toy-like boats dared to rival great ships! But now, the toy-like boats have either fled to a harbor or they have made a toast for Neptune — they are like a piece of toast that has been soaked in water and has sunk.

"In such storms of fortune, we distinguish the appearance of valor from the reality of valor. When the Sun is shining brightly, a herd of cattle is more annoyed by the gadfly than by the tiger, but when the splitting wind makes the trunks of gnarled oaks flexible so that they bend their knee, forcing the trunk to grow naturally in a bent shape suitable for the building of ships — we call it knee-timber — and when flies have fled to find shelter under the stormy sky, why then the thing of courage, which is roused by the rage of the storm and which sympathizes with rage, replies to chiding fortune in a voice with an accent tuned in the selfsame key. A courageous man reacts vigorously when vigorously challenged."

Ulysses said, "Agamemnon, you are our great commander, the sinew and bone of Greece, the heart of our numbers of soldiers, our soul and only spirit, and in you the temperaments and the minds of all should be embodied. Please hear what I, Ulysses, have to say besides the applause and approbation that I give to the speeches that you, Agamemnon, who are mightiest because of your position and power, and that you, Nestor, who are most revered because of your long and stretched-out life, made. I give applause and approbation to both your speeches, which were such as Agamemnon, the hands of the Greeks should hold up high after they are engraved in brass, and also are such as venerable Nestor, whose hair is streaked with silver, should with a bond of air, as strong as the axle-tree — the Earth — around which the planets and the Heavens revolve, knit all the Greek ears to his experienced tongue. Nestor is such an excellent speaker that he could recite both your speeches and use the waves of sounds to bind Greek ears to the words. Yet may it please you both — you, great Agamemnon, and you, wise Nestor — to hear me, Ulysses, speak."

"Speak, Ulysses, Prince of the island of Ithaca," Agamemnon replied. Using the royal plural, he said, "We are confident that when rank and foulmouthed Thersites opens his dog-like jaws we shall never hear music, intelligence, and divine prophecy. We are even more confident that you will not divide your lips in order to talk unnecessarily about unimportant matters."

Ulysses said, "Troy, which still stands on its foundation, would have fallen and the great Hector's sword would have lacked a master by now, except for these reasons I will explain now. The specialty of rule — the rights of and obligations to authority — has been neglected. Look, many hollow Greek tents stand upon this plain; we have that many hollow — false and unsound — factions.

"Whenever the army general is not like the beehive to whom the foragers for food shall all repair, what honey can be expected? When a person of high degree wears a mask, the men who are the unworthiest appear to be just as high of degree while they are also wearing a mask.

"The Heavens themselves, the planets and this center — the Earth — observe degree, priority and proper place and station, regularity of position, course, proportion, season, form, office and custom, according to their rank. And therefore the glorious Sol — the Sun — in noble eminence is enthroned and set in its sphere amid the other Heavenly bodies. The Sun's medicinal eye corrects the ill aspects of evil astrological planets, and speeds, like the commandment of a King, without check, to good and bad.

"But when the planets wander into an evil and disordered conjunction, what plagues and what portents result! What mutiny and rebellion! What raging of the sea! What shaking of the Earth! What commotion in the winds! What frights, changes, and horrors divert, crack, tear, and uproot the unity and married calm of states and governments quite from their fixed position!

"Oh, when rank is forgotten, rank that is the ladder to all high designs, then enterprise is sick! How could communities, degrees in schools and brotherhoods in cities, peaceful commerce from shores separated by seas, the right of primogeniture and the due of birth, the prerogative of age, crowns, scepters, and laurel wreaths stand in an authentic place except by rank and degree?

"But if you take rank and degree away, if you untune that string, then — hark! — what discord follows! Each thing meets in complete opposition. The waters that are bounded by the shores would lift their bosoms — their waves — higher than the shores and make sodden all this solid globe.

"Strength would be the lord of weakness, the strong would rule the weak, and the rude and violent son would strike his father dead. Might would be right; or rather, might would be right and wrong. Justice weighs in its scales what is right and what is wrong, but without the observance of degree and rank, both right and wrong would lose their names and be forgotten, and the same would happen to justice, too.

"Without the observance of degree and rank, everything becomes subservient to power, power becomes subservient to willfulness, and willfulness becomes subservient to appetite, aka desire.

"Appetite is a universal wolf, and because it is doubly seconded with willfulness and power, it must necessarily make a universal prey, and at last eat up himself. Hungry wolves will kill each other one by one until only one is left. But appetite is so strong that the last wolf left will kill itself.

"Great Agamemnon, this chaos, when degree and rank are suffocated, follows the choking. Chaos necessarily follows the neglect of degree and rank. And because of this neglect of degree and rank, a person who takes a step goes lower, although he intends to climb higher.

"The general is disdained by the man who is one step below him, that man is disdained by the next man, and that next man is disdained by the man beneath him, so every step, following the example of the first step of the man who is sick of his superior, grows to an envious fever of pale and bloodless and jealous rivalry. Each man follows the bad example of the man just above him.

"And it is this fever that keeps Troy from being conquered, not her own sinews. To end a lengthy tale, Troy still stands because of our weakness, not because of her strength."

Nestor said, "Most wisely has Ulysses here revealed the fever that has made all our authority sick."

"You have described the problem, Ulysses, but what is the solution?" Agamemnon asked. "You have described the illness, but what is the remedy?"

Ulysses replied, "The great Achilles, whom public opinion crowns the strongest and the greatest warrior of our army, having his ear full of his airy fame, grows vain of his worth, and he lies in his tent and mocks our plans. With him Patroclus lies upon a lazy bed the livelong day and makes scurrilous jests. And with ridiculous and awkward actions, which — slanderer that he is — Patroclus calls imitations, he mimics us.

"Sometimes, great Agamemnon, he assumes your supreme position, and, like a strutting actor on a stage, whose imagination lies in his hamstrings, and who thinks it wonderful to hear the wooden dialogue and the wooden sound that his long strides make on the wooden stage — he pretends to be your greatness and acts with such a to-be-pitied and over-strained performance. And when he speaks, it is like a metal bell being ground down to tune it — the words are unfitting and even if they were to come from the tongue of Typhon, a mythological monster who roared with a hundred mouths, they would seem to be hyperbolic.

"At this musty and moldy stuff, the huge Achilles, lolling on his bed, which is pressed with his weight, laughs out a loud applause from his deep chest and cries, 'Excellent! It is exactly Agamemnon! Now play Nestor for me — hem, and stroke your beard, as if he were preparing to make some oration.' Once that is done, and Patroclus has portrayed Nestor as nearly accurate as the extreme ends of parallel lines are near to each other, or as like Nestor as the ugly and deformed Vulcan is like his wife — Venus, the goddess of sexual passion — godly Achilles continually cries, 'Excellent! It is Nestor exactly. Now play Nestor again for me, Patroclus. This time show him arming himself in response to a night alarm.'

"And then, truly, the frail defects of age must be the subject of a scene of mirth. Patroclus coughs and spits, and fumbles while putting on his gorget — armor for the throat — with palsied, shaking hands. His hands tremble as he puts in the rivet holding the pieces of the gorget together and then accidentally pulls out the rivet. Sir Valor — Achilles — dies laughing. He cries, 'Oh, enough, Patroclus; stop, or give me ribs of steel! I shall split all my ribs with the pleasure of my laughing.'

"And in this fashion, all our abilities, gifts, natures, shapes, individual and group virtues of great merit, achievements, plots and plans, orders, preventions and defensive maneuvers, exhortations to do battle, or diplomatic speeches to arrange a truce, success or loss, what is or is not, serves as stuff for these two to mock."

Nestor said, "And in the imitation of these two — Achilles and Patroclus — who, as Ulysses says, opinion crowns with an authoritative voice — many are infected. Ajax is grown self-willful, and he bears his head in such a rein, in fully as proud a place as broad-chested Achilles. He keeps to his tent like him. He gives feasts to his supporters; he rails against our management of the war, he is as bold as an oracle, and he sets on Thersites, who is a villain whose gall coins slanders as quickly as a mint makes coins. Thersites compares us to dirt, and he weakens and discredits our exposed position, however thickly hemmed in with danger we are."

Ulysses said, "They censure our policy, and they call it cowardice. They believe that wisdom is not relevant in war, they obstruct foresight and planning, and they value no action except that of physical fighting. The quiet and intellectual people, who plan how many soldiers shall strike the enemy in battle, who decide when the time is right and everything is properly prepared to give the best chance of victory, and who know by careful scouting the enemies' number and strength — why, this has not a finger's dignity to them. They call this bed-work, map-making, armchair strategy. They value more highly the battering ram that batters down the wall, because of the battering ram's great swing and its violent, heavy blows, than the engineer who made the battering ram, or those people who with the fineness of their souls and intellect guide the use of the battering ram."

Nestor said, "Let all this be granted, and we can conclude that the horse of Achilles is worth many sons of Thetis."

Achilles was the son of the sea-goddess Thetis.

A trumpet sounded.

"What trumpet is that?" Agamemnon asked. "Go and find out, Menelaus."

Menelaus said, "Someone has come from Troy."

Aeneas walked over to the Greeks.

Agamemnon asked, "What do you want here before our tent?"

"Is this great Agamemnon's tent?" Aeneas asked. "Please tell me."

"Yes, it is," Agamemnon replied.

"May one who is a herald and a Prince deliver a fair and courteous message to his Kingly ears?" Aeneas asked.

"Yes, you can, with a guarantee that you will not be hurt — a guarantee that is stronger than Achilles' arm," Agamemnon said. "You can deliver your message in front of all the Greek leaders who with one voice call Agamemnon head and general."

"That is fair permission and strong security," Aeneas replied. "How may a stranger to those most imperial looks know them from the eyes of other mortals? How can I tell who is Agamemnon?"

"How!" Agamemnon asked. He was surprised that Aeneas could not tell that he was Agamemnon, leader of the Greek warriors.

"Yes," Aeneas replied. "I ask so that I might awaken reverence and put on a face full of respect, and bid my cheek to be ready with a blush as modest as morning with its blushing dawn when she coldly eyes the youthful Phoebus Apollo the Sun-god as he begins to drive his Sun-chariot across the sky. Which of you is that god in office, that god who guides men? Which of you is the high and mighty Agamemnon?"

Using the royal plural, Agamemnon said, "This Trojan scorns us; or else the men of Troy are ceremonious courtiers who are full of formal etiquette."

Aeneas replied, "When the Trojans are unarmed and not at war, they are courtiers as generous, as courtly, and as debonair as bowing Angels; that's their fame and reputation in peace. But when they need to be soldiers, they have venomous anger, good arms, strong joints, and true swords, and with Jove willing, they are unequalled in courage. But peace, Aeneas. Be quiet, Trojan. Lay your finger on your lips! Praise is worth nothing if the praised person is himself doing the praising, but when the grumbling enemy praises, that is the praise that gets talked about; that praise, solely and surely, is real and leads to fame and good reputation."

Agamemnon asked, "Sir, you man of Troy, do you call yourself Aeneas?"

"Yes, Greek, that is my name."

"Please state what your business is here."

"Sir, pardon me; my business here is for Agamemnon's ears to hear."

"He hears privately nothing that comes from Troy," Agamemnon said.

"I have not come from Troy to whisper and talk confidentially to him," Aeneas replied. "I brought a trumpeter to awaken his ears so that he will pay close attention, and after his ears are awakened I will speak."

"Speak as frankly and freely as the wind. It is not Agamemnon's sleeping hour. That you shall know, Trojan, he is awake, he tells you so himself — I am Agamemnon."

"Trumpeter, blow loud," Aeneas said. "Send your brass voice through all these lazy tents, and every Greek of mettle, let him know that Troy's message shall fairly be spoken aloud."

The trumpet sounded.

Aeneas said, "We have, great Agamemnon, here in Troy a Prince named Hector — Priam is his father — who in this dull and long-continued truce has grown rusty. He ordered me to take a trumpeter, and to speak this message. Kings, Princes, lords! If there is one among the fairest of Greece who holds his honor higher than his ease, who seeks his praise more than he fears his peril, who knows his valor and does not know his fear, who loves his woman more than is shown by the profession of sweet nothings to her own lips, and who dares to avow her beauty and her worth in other arms than hers, by fighting for her — to him Hector makes this challenge.

"Hector, in view of the Trojans and of the Greeks, shall make it good, or do his best to prove it by arms, that he has a lady who is wiser, fairer, and truer than any woman any Greek ever held in his arms. Tomorrow, Hector will with his trumpet call midway between your tents and the walls of Troy to rouse a Greek who is true in love to come and fight him.

"If any Greek comes and fights him, Hector shall honor that Greek; if no Greek comes and fights him, he'll say in Troy when he returns that the Greek dames are sunburnt and are not worth a splinter from a lance. That is my message."

"This message shall be told to the lovers in our army, Lord Aeneas," Agamemnon replied. "If none of them has that kind of soul, then we left them all at home, but we are soldiers, and may that soldier prove to be a mere recreant who means not to be in love, has not been in love, or is not in love! If one of our soldiers is, or has been, or means to be in love, then that one meets Hector; if no one else will fight him, I am the man who will fight him."

Nestor said, "Tell Hector about Nestor, who was a man when Hector's grandfather was still being breastfed. Nestor is old now, but if there is not in our Greek army one noble man who has one spark of fire to fight Hector on behalf of his loved one, tell Hector from me that I'll hide my silver beard behind the gold beaver of a helmet and in my forearm-protecting armor I will put this withered arm, and when I meet him to fight him, I will tell him that my lady was fairer than his grandmother and as chaste as any woman in the world.

Although Hector's youth is in flood, I'll back up what I tell him with my three remaining drops of blood."

"May the Heavens now forbid such scarcity of youth!" Aeneas said.

"Amen," Ulysses said.

"Fair Lord Aeneas, let me shake your hand," Agamemnon said. "To our pavilion I shall lead you, sir. Achilles shall hear your message and so shall each lord of Greece; your message shall be announced from tent to tent. You yourself shall feast with us before you go and find welcome from a noble foe."

All began to leave except Ulysses.

Ulysses hissed, "Nestor!"

Nestor stayed behind with Ulysses; they were alone together.

"What do you want, Ulysses?"

"I have the beginning of an idea in my brain; stay with me for a while and help me make it a mature idea."

"What is your young idea?"

"This is it. Blunt wedges split hard knots. In our camp we have a hard knot that we must split without the use of subtlety. The seed of pride that was in Achilles has fully matured and is developing its own seeds that can be sown in others. The pride that rank Achilles has must now be cropped and cut down unless it releases its seeds and breed a nursery of similar evil in other warriors who will tower over and overpower all of us."

"True, but what can we do in response?"

"This challenge that the gallant Hector sends, however it is expressed as a challenge to any Greek warrior, is in reality a challenge to Achilles only."

"That is correct," Nestor said. "The object of the challenge is evident and obvious. We see that in the details."

It was widely known in the Greek camp that Achilles was in love with a Trojan woman: one of Hector's sisters.

"By looking at the details, we can see the big picture," Nestor said. "A row of little numbers in an accounting ledger can add up to a sum of great wealth. When the challenge is publicly announced, there is no doubt that Achilles, even if his brain were as barren as the sandbanks of Libya — though, Apollo knows, Achilles' brain is dry and barren enough — will, with great speed of judgment, yes, with celerity, realize that Hector is explicitly challenging him."

"And Achilles will answer the challenge and fight Hector, don't you think?" Ulysses asked.

"Yes, and it is most fitting for Achilles to fight Hector. Who else may you get to oppose Hector and defeat him and gain — not lose — honor, except for Achilles? Although this will be a recreational combat that is not to the death, yet in the duel much reputation is at stake. For here in this duel the Trojans will taste our dearest repute with their finest palate — their best warrior will fight our best warrior. Believe me, Ulysses, our reputation shall be oddly balanced in this trivial action — our reputation as warriors will be at risk in this duel, although it involves only one of our warriors.

"Although the duel involves only two particular warriors, it shall give a reputation of good or bad to the general body of soldiers. A table of contents is small compared to the entire book, but the table of contents is a good indicator of the worth of the entire volume. In the table of contents is seen the baby figure of the giant mass of things to come at large. A victory in this duel can make our warriors think that a victory in the war is likely. It is supposed that the man who meets Hector is chosen by us to meet him. Because all of us choose our champion, we know that the choice is made on the basis of merit — naturally, we would choose our best warrior to fight Hector. Since we would choose a warrior whom we consider our best — a warrior who figuratively is boiled so that his virtues are concentrated — if that warrior were to lose the duel, then the conquering Trojans will be heartened and will form a strong, steely opinion of themselves. Once warriors have such good morale and such a good opinion of themselves, then their limbs become weapons that are no less effective than the swords and bows that the limbs direct."

Ulysses replied, "Pardon me for what I have to say because I am going to say something contrary to what you just said. I conclude that it is meet — fitting — Achilles does not meet — fight — Hector. We must not allow Achilles to fight Hector in a duel. Let us, like merchants, show our foulest wares, and think, perhaps, they'll sell; if they don't sell, the luster of the better wares that we have yet to show shall show all the better. Let a warrior worse than Achilles fight Hector. Perhaps he'll win. If he does not, we can say that we have better warriors who did not fight Hector. Do not consent that Hector and Achilles ever meet in a duel because both our honor and our shame in this are dogged with two bad consequences."

"I don't see them with my old eyes," Nestor said. "What are they?"

"The two bad consequences follow from this fact: Either Achilles will win the duel or he will be defeated.

"Whatever glory our Achilles wins from Hector, we all would share with him, if he were not proud. But Achilles is already too insolent, and we would be better off being parched in the African Sun than in the pride and bitter scorn of his eyes. That is what would happen if he defeated Hector.

"But if Hector were to defeat Achilles, why then the reputation of our entire army is hurt because the reputation of our best warrior has been tainted.

"Let us avoid both bad consequences by making a lottery, and, through use of a trick, we will have the blockheaded Ajax draw the lot to fight with Hector. Among ourselves we will praise him for being our best warrior because that will be a dose of medicine for the great Myrmidon — Achilles — who basks in loud applause, and it will make him lower his helmet crest that curves prouder than the rainbow along which the goddess Iris travels.

"If the dull, brainless Ajax should come safely away from the duel, we will dress him up with shouts of acclamation. If he fails and loses the duel, we will still have the opinion that we have better men than him — better men who could have defeated Hector.

"But, hit or miss, whether Ajax wins or loses, the outcome of our project will have this consequence: Our employing Ajax in this way will pluck down Achilles' plumes — Achilles will become less proud."

"Ulysses, now I begin to relish your advice, and I will give a taste of it forthwith to Agamemnon. Let's go to him right away. Two curs shall tame each other. Pride alone must provoke the mastiffs on, as if it were their bone."

CHAPTER 2

— 2.1 —

Ajax and Thersites met in the Greek camp.

"Thersites!" Ajax called.

Ignoring Ajax, Thersites said to himself, "Agamemnon, what if he had boils? Fully all over his body, generally, since he is a general?"

"Thersites!"

"And suppose those boils did run and ooze pus. Let us say they did. Wouldn't the general run then? The general would run with ooze, and the general body of soldiers would run away in fright. Wouldn't that be a botchy core? Wouldn't that be the infected center of a boil? Wouldn't that be a corps of soldiers who were unwilling to fight?"

"Dog!" Ajax called.

"Then would come some matter from him; I see none coming from him now," Thersites said.

He was punning. "Matter" referred to the pus that would ooze from the boil. "Matter" also meant "intelligence." Thersites saw no pus oozing from Agamemnon; he also saw nothing intelligent coming from him.

"You bitch-wolf's son, can't you hear me?" Ajax said. He hit Thersites while saying, "Since you can't hear me, feel me."

"May the plague of Greece fall upon you, you mongrel beef-witted lord!" Thersites said.

The plague sometimes fell upon the crowded Greek camp. Being ill spirited as always, Thersites wanted Ajax — whom he called a mongrel because Ajax' father was Greek and his mother was Trojan — to get the plague. Thersites also called Ajax "beef-witted" because eating beef was reputed to lower the eater's intelligence.

"Speak then, you moldiest leaven, speak," Ajax said. "I will beat you until you cease being ugly and instead become handsome."

"It's much more likely that my criticisms of you will make you intelligent and holy," Thersites said, "but, I think, your horse will sooner memorize an oration than you learn a prayer by heart. You can strike me, can't you? I call down a red plague on your sorry-ass tricks!"

"Toadstool, tell me about the proclamation," Ajax said.

Ajax called Thersites "toadstool" because Thersites' words tended to be poisonous like a toadstool. The insult also included the sense of "toad's excrement."

"Do you think I have no sense, and therefore you can strike me thus?"

"Tell me about the proclamation!"

"You are proclaimed a fool, I think."

"Do not insult me, porcupine, do not; my fingers itch for a fight."

Ajax' intelligence was lacking; sometimes his insults backfired on him. If Ajax' fingers were itching, the pain caused by the porcupine's quills would stop the itching.

"I wish you itched from head to foot and I had the task of scratching you; I would make you the loathsomest scab in Greece."

Thersites was punning on "scab," one meaning of which was "loathsome fellow."

He continued, "When you go forth in the battle incursions, you strike as slowly as the other soldiers."

"I say, tell me about the proclamation!"

"You grumble and rail every hour about Achilles, and you are as full of envy of his greatness as Cerberus is of Proserpine's beauty, yes, and your envy makes you bark at Achilles."

Cerberus was the three-headed dog that guarded Hades, Land of the Dead. Proserpine was the beautiful goddess who was Queen of Hades. Cerberus, the ugliest thing in Hades, envied Proserpine, the most beautiful being in Hades.

"Mistress Thersites!" Ajax said, attempting to insult Thersites by calling him a woman.

"You should strike Achilles!" Thersites continued.

"Cob loaf!"

A cob loaf was a bun — a round loaf or lump of bread.

Thersites said, "Achilles would pound you into pieces with his fist, just as a sailor breaks a hard biscuit."

Ajax hit Thersites while shouting, "You cur! You son of a whore!"

"Do carry on," Thersites said sarcastically.

"You stool for a witch!" Ajax shouted.

Thersites was a jester. Sometimes, a jester carried a monkey on his back. Ajax was saying that a witch could replace the monkey and sit on Thersites' back. In addition, Ajax was calling Thersites a witch's excrement. A stool was also a seat on which one sat while using a chamberpot, and so a stool was a privy. Sometimes, Ajax' insults backfired on him. He had just called Thersites a privy, but "Ajax" is similar to "a jakes," and a jakes is a privy.

"Keep it up," Thersites, who realized that Ajax' joke had backfired, said. "You sodden-witted lord! You alcohol-crazed lord! You have no more brain than I have in my elbows! An *assinego* — Spanish for 'little ass' — may tutor you, you scurvy-valiant, heartily contemptible ass! You are here only to thrash Trojans; and you are bought and sold among those of any wit, like a barbarian slave. If you continue to beat me, I will begin at your heel, and tell you what you are by inches, you thing of no feelings and sensitivity, you!"

"You dog!"

"You scurvy lord!"

Ajax beat him while shouting, "You cur!"

"You are Mars' idiot," Thersites said. "Keep it up, rude man. You camel, keep it up, you beast of burden."

Achilles and Patroclus walked over to them.

"Why, how are you now, Ajax?" Achilles said. "Why are you acting like this? Hello, Thersites! What's the matter, man?"

"Do you see this man there?" Thersites asked, pointing to Ajax.

"Yes," Achilles replied. "What's the matter?"

"No, look at him," Thersites said.

"I am. What's the matter?"

"No, look at him well and closely."

"'Well'!" Achilles said. "Why, I do."

"But yet you are not looking well upon him; for whosoever you take him to be, he is Ajax," Thersites said.

Thersites was punning on "Ajax" and "a jakes," and he was saying that Achilles was not looking well upon Ajax because he did not realize Ajax was a privy.

"I know that, fool," Achilles replied.

Pretending that Achilles had said, "I know that fool," Thersites replied, "Yes, but that fool does not know himself."

"Therefore I beat you," Ajax said, unwittingly agreeing that he was a fool.

"Lo, lo, lo, lo, what tiny amounts of wit he utters!" Thersites said. Putting his hands to his head and mimicking an ass' ears, he added, "His verbal sallies have ears thus long. I have beat his brain more than he has beat my bones. I can buy nine sparrows for a penny, and his *pia mater* — his brain — is not worth the ninth part of a sparrow. Achilles, I'll tell you what I say of this lord — Ajax — who wears his wit in his belly and his guts in his head."

"What?" Achilles asked.

"I say, this Ajax —" Thersites began.

Ajax raised his hand as if he were going to hit Thersites.

"Don't, good Ajax," Achilles said.

"— has not as much wit —"

Achilles grabbed Ajax and kept him from hitting Thersites, saying, "No, Ajax. I must hold you and prevent you from hitting Thersites."

"— as will stop the eye of Helen's needle, for whom he comes to fight."

One meaning of the eye of Helen's needle was her vagina.

"Peace, fool!" Achilles said. "Shut up!"

"I would have peace and quietness, but the fool will not," Thersites said. He pointed at Ajax and said, "The fool is he there — that he. Look at him there."

Ajax began, "Oh, you damned cur! I shall —"

Achilles interrupted him: "Will you set your wit against a fool's?"

"No, I assure you," Thersites said, "for a Fool's wit will shame Ajax' wit."

Many Fools — professional jesters — in fact were wise, or at least clever.

"Speak good words, Thersites," Patroclus said. "Be nice."

"What's the quarrel between you two?" Achilles asked Ajax.

"I bade the vile owl — this vile bird of omen — to tell me the content of the proclamation, and he rails upon and insults me."

"I am not your servant," Thersites said.

"Whatever," Ajax said.

"I serve here voluntarily."

"Your last service was sufferance and involved suffering; it was not voluntary," Achilles said. "No man is beaten voluntarily. Ajax was just now the volunteer, and you were under an impress — he drafted you to be beaten without your permission."

"That is true," Thersites replied. "A great deal of your intelligence, too, lies in your muscles, or else I have been listening to liars."

He added sarcastically, "Hector shall have a great catch, if he knocks out either of your brains. It would be as good as cracking a moldy nutshell that contained no nut."

"Are you saying that about me as well as about Ajax, Thersites?" Achilles asked.

"Ulysses and old Nestor, whose wit was moldy before your grandsires had nails on their toes, yoke you as if you were draft-oxen and make you plow up the wars. They order you about and make you do heavy fighting in the war."

"What!" Achilles said.

"Yes, indeed," Thersites said. "Pull that load, Achilles! Pull it, Ajax! Pull!"

"I shall cut out your tongue," Ajax said.

"It doesn't matter," Thersites replied. "I shall speak as much as you afterwards."

Ajax was a warrior, not a diplomat; he also was not an intelligent man. Thersites would speak as much sense as Ajax even if Thersites' tongue were cut out. And if a person makes sounds that are nonsense, is that person speaking?

"No more words, Thersites," Patroclus said. "Peace!"

"I will hold my peace when Achilles' brooch, or should I say 'brach,' bids me, shall I?" Thersites said.

Both "brooch" and "brach" were insults. A brooch is worn on clothing — it hangs on clothing. Thersites was calling Patroclus Achilles' hanger-on. A "brach" is a female dog, a bitch. Thersites was calling Patroclus Achilles' bitch — his male prostitute.

"There's an insult for you, Patroclus," Achilles said.

"I will see you hanged, like clodpoles, like blockheads, before I come any more to your tents," Thersites said. "I will keep myself among people of wit and intelligence and leave the faction and the company of fools."

He exited.

"A good riddance," Patroclus said.

Achilles said to Ajax, "Sir, it is proclaimed through all our host of soldiers that Hector, by the fifth hour after sunrise, will with a trumpet between our tents and Troy tomorrow morning call some knight to arms who has a stomach to fight and such a knight who dares to maintain — I know not what. It is trash and doesn't matter. Farewell."

"Farewell," Ajax said, then added, "Who shall answer his challenge and fight him?"

"I don't know," Achilles replied. "A lottery will be held, otherwise Hector knows which man would fight him."

"Oh, meaning you," Ajax said. "I will go and learn more about this."

They exited.

In a room in King Priam's palace in Troy, a council was being held. Priam, Hector, Troilus, Paris, and Helenus attended it and spoke.

King Priam said, "After so many hours, lives, and speeches spent, thus once again Nestor gives us this message from the Greeks: *'Deliver Helen into our hands, and all other damages — such as honor, loss of time, travail and travel, expense, wounds, friends, and what else dear that is consumed in the hot digestion of this war that is as insatiable as a cormorant, a bird of prey — shall be struck off the list of damages and forgotten.'* Hector, what do you have to say about this?"

Hector said, "Though no man less fears the Greeks than I as far as I am personally concerned, yet, revered Priam, no lady has feelings that are more tender and more spongy to suck in the sense of fear for others, and no lady is more ready to cry out 'Who knows what follows?' than Hector is. Peace is wounded by overconfident confidence, but sensible caution is called the beacon and guiding light of the wise — it is the cloth swab that cleans to the bottom of the worst wound. Let Helen go; let her return to the Greeks. Since the first sword was drawn about this question, every tithe-soul, among many thousands of tithes, has been as valuable as Helen; I am referring to the Trojan soldiers who have died in the war over Helen. If we have lost so many tenths of our soldiers, to guard a thing — Helen — that is not ours and is not worth to us, even if she were Trojan, the value of one tithe, what merit is in the argument against yielding her up? I say that Helen is not worth the death of even one Trojan soldier, and yet one tenth of our soldiers have died in the war over her."

"Wrong, you are wrong, my brother!" Troilus said. "Do you weigh the worth and honor of a King as great as our revered father in a scale that measures only ounces and not great weights? Will you use useless counters to add up the immeasurability of his vastness? Will you buckle in a waist most fathomless with spans and inches that are as diminutive as fears and arguments? Be ashamed, for godly shame!"

Troilus believed that the deaths of so many Trojan soldiers were justified. To give up Helen would cause his and Hector's father, King Priam, to lose honor.

Helenus said to Troilus, "It's no wonder that you bite so sharply at reasons since you are so empty of them. Are you saying that our father should not govern the great command of his affairs with reasons? Your speech has no reasons that tell him to govern that way. A ruler should use reason and arguments to determine how best to rule; in your speech you have shown no reason, no arguments, and no concern for ruling well."

Troilus replied, "You are for dreams and slumbers, brother priest; you fur your gloves with reason. You use reason and reasons to make your life more comfortable. Here are your reasons to give Helen back to the Greeks: You know an enemy intends you harm, and you know that an employed sword is perilous. Reason flees the object that causes harm. Who marvels then that when Helenus sees a Greek and the Greek's sword he attaches the wings of reason on his heels and flees like chidden Mercury from Jove, or like a star falling from its Heavenly sphere?"

Mercury was the fleet messenger-god who served Jove, aka Jupiter, King of the gods. Mercury had wings on his ankles, which made him fast. He was mischievous and did such things as steal the cattle of his fellow god Apollo, which resulted in Mercury being chidden by Jove.

Troilus continued, "If we talk about reason, let's shut our gates and sleep. We won't need to go out on the battlefield and fight; instead, we can stay home and take naps. Manhood and honor would have the hearts of cowardly hares, if they would make fat their thoughts by cramming them with reason. Reason and prudence make men cowardly and youthful vigor dejected."

Hector said to Troilus, "Brother, Helen is not worth what she costs us to hold her."

Troilus replied, "What is the worth of anything, except the value people put on it?"

"But value dwells not in a particular, subjective desire," Hector said. "Something gets its value and worth from itself — its objective value and worth — as well as from what value and worth a person prizes it as. The objective worth and value are more important than the subjective worth and value. It is mad idolatry to make the religious service greater than the god; the will loves and desires foolishly when the will is inclined to attach value to the thing that it — to its own harm — loves and desires, when it has no objective perception of the value of the thing it desires."

A person's will is that person's desire. Free will means that we can choose whether or not to try to satisfy our desire. In some cases, reason will tell us that a certain desire is bad and moral reasoning will tell us that we ought not to try to satisfy that desire. In other cases, reason will tell us that a certain desire is good and moral reasoning will tell us that we ought to try to satisfy that desire.

Part of what Hector was saying is that good and bad are objective. Something is really good or it is really bad, and whether it is good or bad is not a matter of opinion. Part of what Troilus was saying is that good and bad are subjective. Something is good if you think it is good; something is bad if you think it is bad.

Many people believe that good and bad, and right and wrong, are objective — not dependent upon opinion, and incumbent upon all rational beings. According to objectivism, moral values and principles do not depend upon a particular person's opinions. According to objectivism, moral values and principles allow us to judge ethical statements such as "Murder is morally wrong" as either true or false.

Nevertheless, objectivists realize that some things are subjective. You and I may feel a breeze blowing. You may think that breeze feels cold; I may think that the breeze feels warm. Both of us are right. The breeze feels cold to you, and it feels warms to me. However, the temperature of the breeze is objective; if the temperature is 68 degrees Fahrenheit, then the temperature is not 48 degrees Fahrenheit.

Troilus replied, "Suppose that I take today a wife, and my deliberate choice of a wife is led on and guided by my will. My eyes and ears inflamed my will; my wife is beautiful and has a pleasing voice. My sense of sight and my sense of hearing are two experienced pilots that travel between the dangerous shores of will and judgment. I saw and heard a woman, I desired her, and I married her. Suppose that time passes and I no longer desire the woman I made my wife? How may I reject her, now that I no longer desire her? After all, she is my wife; I chose to marry her. If I am an honorable man, I cannot evade the decision I made and flinch away from her. We do not return silks to the merchant after we have soiled the silks, and we do not throw away all the leftover food simply because we are now full. Instead, we see first if we can use any of the leftover food rather than throwing it away or feeding it to animals.

"It was thought fitting that Paris should do some vengeance on the Greeks. Your breath and voices of full consent bellied his sails and helped him sail to Greece to get that vengeance."

The vengeance was retribution for an act committed many years earlier. The gods Apollo and Neptune built the walls of Troy for King Laomedon, who then refused to pay them the wages he had promised. To get vengeance, Neptune sent a sea monster to Troy. Soothsayers said that if Hesione, the daughter of King Laomedon and the sister of the future King Priam, were sacrificed to the sea monster, then Troy would no longer suffer from the sea monster. Hercules, a Greek, came to Troy during his travels, and said that he would kill the sea monster and save Hesione in return for a reward. Hercules killed the sea monster, but King Laomedon refused to give him the reward, so Hercules kidnapped Hesione and gave her to Telamon, a Greek King. They became the parents of Ajax. To get vengeance for Hercules' kidnapping of Hesione, Paris went to Greece and kidnapped Helen, the wife of Menelaus, King of Sparta.

Troilus continued, "The seas and winds, old enemies, made a truce and gave Paris good service. He visited the ports he desired, and for an old aunt — Hesione, Paris' aunt — whom the Greeks held captive, Paris brought back to Troy a Greek Queen, Helen, whose youth and freshness make the god Apollo seem wrinkled, and make the fresh morning seem stale.

"Why do we keep Helen? The Greeks keep our aunt. Is Helen worth keeping? Why, Helen is a pearl whose price has launched more than a thousand ships, and turned crowned Kings into merchants who want to purchase that pearl.

"If you'll affirm that it was wise that Paris went to Greece — as you necessarily must, for you all cried, 'Go, go,' and if you'll confess that he brought home a noble prize — as you necessarily must, for you all clapped your hands and cried, 'Inestimable!' — why do you now berate the outcome of your proper wisdom, and do a deed that fortune never did, which is to berate and rate as worthless the thing that you prized as being richer than sea and land?

"Oh, it is a very base theft when we are afraid to keep something that we have stolen! But we are thieves, and we are unworthy of the thing we stole — we disgraced the Greeks in their own country by stealing that thing, yet we are afraid in our own country to justify that theft!"

Outside the council chamber, Cassandra screamed, "Cry, Trojans, cry!"

Cassandra was one of King Priam's daughters. She had agreed to sleep with the god Apollo if he gave her the gift of prophecy, but after he gave her that gift, she reneged on her promise. Apollo was unable to take his gift back, but he gave her another "gift": Her prophecies would be true, but no one would believe them until after they came true. Rather than believing her prophecies, her hearers would consider her mad — insane.

"What noise is this?" Priam asked. "What shriek is this?"

"It is our mad sister," Troilus replied. "I recognize her voice."

"Cry, Trojans!" Cassandra screamed.

"It is Cassandra," Hector confirmed.

Cassandra, raving, entered the council chamber.

"Cry, Trojans, cry! Lend me ten thousand eyes, and I will fill them with prophetic tears!"

"Peace, sister, peace!" Hector said. "Be quiet, sister!"

"Virgins and boys, middle-aged men and wrinkled elders, soft infants who can do nothing but cry, add to my clamors!" Cassandra screamed. "Let us pay now a part of that mass of moans to come. Cry, Trojans, cry! Employ your eyes by creating tears! Troy must cease to exist, and our beautiful palace will no longer stand. Our firebrand brother, Paris, burns us all."

When Queen Hecuba was pregnant with Paris, she dreamed that she gave birth to a firebrand — a torch — that burned the city of Troy.

Cassandra screamed, "Cry, Trojans, cry! A Helen and a woe! Cry, cry! Either Troy burns, or else you let Helen go!"

Cassandra ran from the council chamber.

Hector said, "Now, youthful Troilus, do not these high strains of divination in our sister create in you some feelings of remorse? Or is your blood so madly hot that no discourse of reason, nor fear of a bad outcome in a bad cause, can diminish the hotness of your blood?"

Troilus replied, "Why, brother Hector, we may not think the justness of each act is formed only by its outcome, and we may not even once lessen the courage of our minds just because Cassandra's mad. Her brainsick raptures cannot make distasteful the goodness of a quarrel in which all our honor is engaged — our honor makes that quarrel gracious and righteous. For my private part, I am no more personally affected than all Priam's sons, and may

Jove forbid that there should be done among us such things as might convince the least courageous among us not to fight for and keep Helen!"

Paris said, "If we were to do that, the world might find guilty of levity my undertakings as well as your counsels. But I call on the gods to give evidence that your full consent gave wings to my inclination to get vengeance, and I swear to the gods that your full consent cut off all fears accompanying so dire a project.

"For what, alas, can these my arms do by themselves? What fighting ability is in one man's valor that can stand the assault and enmity of those this quarrel would excite? Yet, I protest, if I alone were to experience the difficulties and if I had as ample power as I have will and desire, then I, Paris, would never retract what I have done, nor would I lose courage in the endeavor."

Priam said, "Paris, you speak like one drunk on your sweet delights. You still have the sweet honey, but these men have the bitter gall, so your being valiant is not at all praiseworthy."

Paris replied, "Sir, I propose not merely to keep for myself the pleasures such a beauty brings with it, for I want to have the soil of Helen's fair rape wiped off, by honorably keeping her."

One meaning of the word "rape" is "violent seizure" — Paris had kidnapped Helen. In a moment he would refer to Helen as "the ransacked Queen" — the word "ransack" means "plundered."

Paris continued, "What treason would it be to the ransacked Queen, what disgrace would it be to your great reputations and what shame would it be to me to now deliver her possession up on terms of base and dishonorable compulsion! It would be a disgrace for us to return Helen simply because we were forced to! Can it be that so degenerate a strain of disposition as this should once set foot in your generous bosoms?

"Not even the meanest and lowest man in our faction is without a heart to dare or a sword to draw when Helen is defended, nor is there anyone so noble that his life would be ill bestowed and his death would be without fame where Helen is the subject. So then, I say, well may we fight for her whom, we know well, the world's large spaces cannot parallel. The world does not have Helen's equal."

Hector said, "Paris and Troilus, you have both spoken well, and on the cause and question now in hand have given a commentary, but you have done that superficially. You are much like the young men whom Aristotle thought unfit to learn moral philosophy. The arguments you make contribute more to increasing the hot passion of distempered blood than they do to making a fair determination between right and wrong that is free from the influence of pleasure and revenge, which have ears deafer than the ears of adders to the voice of any true and unbiased decision. Nature craves that all dues be rendered to their owners. Now, what family relationship in all humanity is closer than a wife is to her husband? In case this law of nature is corrupted through sexual appetite, and in case great minds, because of biased indulgence given to their paralyzed wills, resist that law of nature, there is a law in each well-ordered nation to curb those raging sexual appetites that are most wanton and rebellious.

"If Helen then is the wife of Sparta's King, as we know she is, these moral laws of nature and of nations speak loudly to have her returned to her husband. To persist in doing wrong does not extenuate that wrong, but instead makes it much heavier and more serious.

"My — Hector's — opinion is truly what I have just said — Helen ought to be returned to her husband. Nevertheless, my spirited brothers, I am inclined to agree that we resolve to always keep Helen because this is a cause that has no mean consequences for our collective and individual honors. We will gain honor if we fight to keep Helen. Glory and honor are objectively valuable."

"Why, there you touched upon the life of our undertaking," Troilus said. "If we did not favor glory more than the performance of our aroused anger, I would not wish a single drop of Trojan blood to be spent in keeping Helen. But, worthy Hector, Helen is a theme — a reason to take action — of honor and renown. She is a spur to valiant and magnanimous deeds. The courage of those deeds may beat down our foes now, and it may achieve for us fame in the times to come — fame that will canonize and immortalize us. People will remember our names and our brave deeds long after we are dead. I say this because I presume that brave Hector would not lose so rich an opportunity for achieving glory as now so promisingly smiles upon the forehead of this action even if he could get the wide world's revenue instead of glory."

"I am on your side, you valiant offspring of great Priam," Hector said. "I have sent a roistering challenge to the lifeless and quarreling nobles of the Greeks. I was informed that their great general, Agamemnon, slept while factious rivalry and ambitious conflict into his army crept. My challenge, I presume, will awaken him."

Thersites stood in front of Achilles' tent in the Greek camp and talked to himself. Thersites had been Ajax' Fool, but now he was Achilles' Fool. Fools, aka jesters, had the freedom to satirize other people. Much of their job was to be amusing, but they could be very critical.

"How are you doing now, Thersites! What! I see that you are lost in the labyrinth of your fury! Shall the elephant-like — slow and proud — Ajax win the day and defeat me? He beats me, and I rail at him. Oh, is this worthy satisfaction? I wish it were otherwise; I would like to beat him while he railed at me. By God, I'll learn to make spells and raise Devils, but I'll see that my spiteful curses have some kind of result.

"Then there's Achilles, an exceptional plotter and contriver! If Troy cannot be taken until these two — Achilles and Ajax — undermine it, the walls will stand until they fall by themselves.

"Oh, you great thunder-thrower of Olympus, forget that you are Jove, the King of gods, and you, Mercury, lose all the serpentine craft of your caduceus — your wand with the two serpents wound around it — if you do not take that little little — less than little — wit away from them that they have! They have less than little intelligence — take it away from them! Even short-armed ignorance — ignorance has short arms and therefore little intellectual reach — itself knows that their intelligence is so abundantly scarce that it will not form a plan to deliver a fly from a spider that does not include drawing their massive iron swords and cutting the web.

"After you steal these two men's little intelligence, then take vengeance on the whole camp! I know! Give them the bone-ache — give them syphilis! For that, I think, is the curse belonging to those who war for a placket."

A placket was literally a petticoat, and metaphorically a woman. Another meaning of "placket" was literally a hole in the front of a petticoat, and metaphorically a vagina.

Thersites continued, "I have said my prayers and the Devil Envy says, 'Amen.'"

Thersites was self-aware. He called the curses he uttered "spiteful," and he believed that the Devil Envy approved of his "prayers," aka "curses."

He heard something and said, "What! My Lord Achilles!"

The noise was caused not by Achilles, but by Patroclus, who said, "Who's there? Thersites! Good Thersites, come in and rail. We want to hear you curse and criticize people."

Thersites said, "If I could have remembered a gilt counterfeit, you would not have slipped out of my contemplation."

A gilt counterfeit was a counterfeit coin — one made of brass and then covered with silver or gold. A slang term for such a counterfeit coin was a "slip."

Thersites was saying that if he could have remembered Patroclus, he would have cursed him in his contemplation. Thersites was calling Patroclus a counterfeit man — a homosexual. Thersites regarded Patroclus as a "gilt counterfeit" — metaphorically, he was a gelt, aka gelded or castrated, counterfeit man, aka homosexual.

Thersites continued, "But it does not matter because I can curse you now: thyself upon thyself! The worst curse I can give you is to tell you to keep on being yourself!

"May the common curse of mankind, folly and ignorance, be yours in great abundance! May Heaven bless you by keeping you away from a tutor, and may discipline and learning not come near you! Let your passions be your masters until your death! Don't think rationally about what you ought to do, but instead do whatever you want to do.

"Then if the woman who lays you out and prepares you for burial says that you are a good-looking corpse, I'll be sworn in a court of law and swear that she never shrouded any bodies but those of lepers.

"Amen. Where's Achilles?"

"What, are you devout?" Patroclus asked. "Were you in prayer?"

"Yes," Thersites replied. "I pray that the Heavens hear my prayer!"

Achilles walked onto the scene and asked, "Who's there?"

Patroclus answered, "Thersites, my lord."

"Where? Where?" Achilles asked. Seeing Thersites, he said, "Have you come? Why, my cheese, my digestion, why haven't you served yourself in to my table for so many meals?"

Cheese was served at the end of meals because people thought that cheese aided digestion. Achilles wanted Thersites — his cheese — to entertain him at the end of meals.

Achilles said to Thersites, "Tell me, what is Agamemnon?"

"Your commander, Achilles," Thersites replied. He then said, "Tell me, Patroclus, what is Achilles?"

"Your lord and boss, Thersites," Patroclus replied. "Tell me, please, what are you?"

"I am the person who knows what you are, Patroclus," Thersites replied. "Tell me, Patroclus, what are you?"

"You are the person who said he knows what I am," Patroclus said. "So you tell me what I am."

"Tell us! Tell us!" Achilles said.

"I'll tell what everybody is," Thersites said. "Agamemnon commands Achilles; Achilles is my lord; I am the person who knows what Patroclus is, and Patroclus is a fool."

"You rascal!" Patroclus said.

"Silence, fool!" Thersites said. "I have not finished."

Achilles said to Patroclus, "Thersites is a privileged man."

As a Fool, Thersites was allowed to speak freely and to criticize freely.

Achilles said, "Proceed, Thersites."

Thersites said, "Agamemnon is a fool; Achilles is a fool; Thersites is a Fool, and, as I said before, Patroclus is a fool."

"Explain this," Achilles said. "How did you arrive at this conclusion? Tell us."

Thersites said, "Agamemnon is a fool to try to command Achilles; Achilles is a fool to be commanded by Agamemnon; Thersites is a Fool to serve such a fool as Achilles, and Patroclus is a complete and utter fool."

"Why am I a fool?" Patroclus asked.

"Ask your Creator," Thersites replied. "It is enough for me to know that you are a fool."

Seeing some people coming toward them, Thersites said, "Look. Who is coming here?"

Achilles said, "Patroclus, I'll speak with nobody. Come in with me, Thersites."

Achilles disappeared into his tent.

Thersites said, "Here is such foolishness, such trickery, and such knavery! All this argument is over a cuckold named Menelaus and a whore named Helen."

He added sarcastically, "This is a good quarrel to break up into competing factions over and to bleed to death upon."

He added honestly, "May a skin disease metaphorically spread on the subject! And may war and lechery destroy them all!"

Thersites disappeared into Achilles' tent.

Agamemnon, Ulysses, Nestor, Diomedes, and Ajax walked over to Patroclus.

"Where is Achilles?" Agamemnon asked.

"He is inside his tent, but he is not feeling well, my lord," Patroclus replied.

Using the royal plural, Agamemnon said, "Let it be known to him that we are here. He insulted our messengers, and we are setting aside our prerogatives of rank by visiting him. Let him be told so, lest perhaps he should think that we don't dare bring up the fact of our position or that we don't know our high rank."

"I shall say so to him," Patroclus said. He disappeared into Achilles' tent.

"We saw Achilles just now at the opening of his tent," Ulysses said. "He is not sick."

"Yes, he is sick," Ajax said. "He is lion-sick — that is, he is sick because he has a proud heart. You may call it by the nice term 'melancholy,' if you want to support the man and justify his actions, but, by my head, it is pride that he suffers from and that causes his actions. But why, why? Let Achilles show us the cause. Let him explain why he acts the way he does."

He then asked Agamemnon, "May I have a private word with you, my lord?"

He and Agamemnon went a short distance away and talked.

Nestor asked Ulysses, "What moves Ajax thus to bay and bark at Achilles?"

"Achilles has inveigled Ajax' Fool to stop being Ajax' Fool and instead become Achilles' Fool."

"Ajax' Fool? Who, Thersites?"

"Yes, Thersites."

Nestor said, "Then Ajax will lack matter and content to talk about, if he has lost his argument — that thing that he constantly complains about."

Ulysses replied, "No, because you see, the person is his argument who has his argument: Achilles. Achilles took away Ajax' subject to complain about, and so now Achilles becomes Ajax' subject to everlastingly complain about."

Ulysses was well read. He was alluding to this sentence that appears in Erasmus' *Adaglia*: "*Denique rationonem aut argumentem* Achilleum *vocant, quod sit insuperabile & insolubile.*" This is Latin for "Finally, they call a reason or an argument *Achillean* because it is insuperable and insoluble." Ulysses' knowledge of Erasmus' work is especially impressive because Erasmus lived and wrote centuries after Ulysses had died. Another well-read warrior was Hector, who knew about Aristotle, who lived and wrote centuries after Hector had died.

The traditional date of the fall of Troy is 1184 BCE. Aristotle lived during 384–322 BCE. Desiderius Erasmus lived during 1466–1536 CE.

Nestor said, "It's all the better that Ajax dislikes Achilles. We prefer their fraction to their faction. It's better that they quarrel with each other than unite against us."

He added sarcastically, "It was a strong combination if a fool could disunite it."

The fool meant was the Fool Thersites, but Ajax was another fool — as was Achilles.

"If wisdom does not tie together friends, folly may easily untie them," Ulysses said. "Here comes Patroclus."

Patroclus returned.

"No Achilles is with him," Nestor observed.

"The elephant has joints, but none for courtesy," Ulysses said. "The elephant's legs are legs for necessity, not for bending."

He meant that the elephant, symbol of pride, would bow to no one. Achilles, because of his pride, would not be submissive to Agamemnon.

Patroclus said, "Achilles told me to say to you, Agamemnon, that he is very sorry if anything more than your entertainment and pleasure moved your greatness and these nobles with you to call upon him; he hopes your visit is for no other reasons than for the sake of your health and your digestion, and for an after-dinner's walk."

"Listen to me, Patroclus," Agamemnon said. "We are too well acquainted with these answers: We have heard them before. But his evasion, winged thus swiftly with scorn, cannot outfly our apprehensions. We are not fooled. Achilles has a great reputation, and great are the reasons why we give him that reputation, yet all his virtues, which now he is not displaying, begin to lose their gloss in our eyes. Yes, they — like beautiful fruit in a dirty dish — are likely to be uneaten and to rot.

"Go and tell him that we have come to speak with him. You shall not sin if you say that I think he is over-proud and under-honorable — excessively proud and less than honorable — and that I think his opinion of himself is greater than others' opinion of him, and that I who am a man greater than he is am here witnessing the unsociable aloofness he puts on. I who am greater than he is rein in the holy strength of my command and submit in an obsequious manner to his humorous predominance — to whatever bodily fluid is controlling his actions."

Doctors in this culture believed that the human body had four humors, or vital fluids. Each humor made a contribution to the personality, and for a human being to be sane and healthy, the four humors had to be present in the right amounts. If a man had too much of a certain humor, it would harm his personality and health.

Blood was the sanguine humor. A sanguine man was optimistic.

Phlegm was the phlegmatic humor. A phlegmatic man was calm.

Yellow bile was the choleric humor. A choleric man was angry.

Black bile was the melancholic humor. A melancholic man was gloomy and morose.

The English word "morose" is derived from the Latin word *morosus*, which means "self-willed." A person who is self-willed insists on doing what he or she — in this culture, it is almost always he — wants to do without regard for the feelings of any other people.

Earlier, Ajax had said that other people could call Achilles melancholic if they wished, but he considered Achilles' illness to be excessive pride.

Using the royal plural, Agamemnon continued, "We watch his petulant tantrums, his ebbs, his flows, as if the events and whole management of this war rode on his tide. Go tell him this, and add that if he overestimates his value so much, we'll have nothing to do with him. Instead, we will treat him like a war machine that is not portable and so cannot be moved and used. We will say, 'Let's leave this war machine behind and go to the battle because this war machine cannot go to war: We will give credit to an active dwarf before we will give credit to a sleeping giant.' Tell him we said so."

"I shall," Patroclus said, "and I will bring back his answer quickly."

He disappeared into the tent.

Agamemnon said, "I will not have Achilles' subordinate bring me Achilles' answer. We have come here to speak with him. Ulysses, enter the tent. You bring me Achilles' answer."

Ulysses disappeared into Achilles' tent.

Ajax said to Agamemnon, "What is Achilles more than another man?"

"He is no more than what he thinks he is," Agamemnon replied.

He was acknowledging that Achilles was the greatest warrior among the Greek soldiers. Ajax was a good warrior, but when Achilles fought, Achilles was a better warrior than Ajax.

"Is he so much?" Ajax said. "Don't you think that he thinks he is a better man than I am?"

"Without question," Agamemnon replied.

"Do you agree with his thought, and say he is?"

"No, noble Ajax; you are as strong, as valiant, as wise, no less noble, much more gentle, and altogether more tractable."

Agamemnon was giving credit to Ajax for — so far, at least — taking orders. Achilles was a greater warrior than Achilles, but Ajax was willing — so far, at least — to take orders from Agamemnon.

"Why should a man be proud?" Ajax asked. "How does pride grow? I don't know what pride is."

Agamemnon replied, "Your mind is clearer than Achilles' mind, Ajax, and your virtues are fairer than Achilles' virtues. A man who is proud eats himself up: Pride is its own mirror, its own trumpet, its own chronicle; and whatever praises itself except but in the deed, devours the deed in the praise. Praising one's own deed lessens that deed. It is better when others praise your deed."

"I hate a proud man just as I hate the breeding and multiplying of toads," Ajax said.

Nestor murmured to Diomedes, "Yet Ajax loves himself. Isn't it strange?"

Ulysses returned.

He said, "Achilles will not go to the battlefield tomorrow."

"What's his excuse?" Agamemnon asked.

"He gives none," Ulysses replied. "He continues to float on the stream of his own disposition and pays no attention and gives no respect to the thoughts of other people. He is self-willed and spends his time in self-admiration."

"Why won't he, as we have politely requested, come out of his tent and spend some time with us?"

"He treats as important issues things that are as small as nothing simply because they have been asked," Ulysses said. "He makes a big issue out of trivial things such as people simply asking him for a small courtesy. He is obsessed with his own greatness, and he is so proud that he cannot speak to himself without starting a quarrel. The worth that he imagines himself to have has so heated his blood that the war between his rational mind and his passions makes him like a Kingdom enduring civil war. He is filled with rebellion and rages and batters himself down. What should I say? He is so plaguy proud that the signs of death resulting from his plague of pride cry, 'No recovery.' His pride is like the plague, and all the symptoms he displays make me think that he will not recover from it."

"Let Ajax go and speak to Achilles," Agamemnon said.

He said to Ajax, "Dear lord, go and greet Achilles in his tent. It is said he well respects you, and he will be led at your request a little from himself. If you ask him, he will be less rebellious."

"Agamemnon, don't let Ajax go to Achilles!" Ulysses said. "We'll consecrate the steps that Ajax makes when they go away from — not toward — Achilles. This proud lord who bastes his arrogance with his own fat as if he were basting roast beef with its own juice and who never allows anything in the world to enter his thoughts, except such things as revolve around and concern himself — shall he be worshipped and adored and sucked-up-to by a man whom we regard as being more worthy of worship than he?"

Ulysses was fulsomely praising Ajax. Ulysses, Agamemnon, Nestor, and Diomedes all knew that Achilles was a better warrior than Ajax, and they all knew that Ajax was a greater fool than Achilles — or anyone — but they wanted to build up Ajax so that he would be a rival to Achilles. They wanted Ajax to fight Hector and, if possible, win the duel. They wanted to praise Ajax so highly that Achilles would feel jealous and would come out of his tent and fight again for and take orders from Agamemnon.

Ulysses continued, "No, this thrice worthy and very valiant lord must not so debase his honor, which is nobly acquired; nor would I want him to ass-subjugate his own merit, despite how amply titled with complimentary epithets Achilles is, by going to Achilles. If he were to go to Achilles, that would only fatten more Achilles' already obese pride, and it would add more coals to Cancer when the zodiacal sign burns by entertaining great Hyperion."

The Sun — the Titan Helios, whose father is Hyperion — enters the part of the zodiac devoted to Cancer when the summer solstice occurs in late June, when the weather in most of the northern hemisphere is already hot and will soon grow hotter.

Ulysses continued, "This lord go to Achilles! May Jupiter forbid that, and may Jupiter say, 'No, Achilles shall go to this lord'!"

Nestor murmured to Diomedes, "Oh, this is wonderful; Ulysses is manipulating Ajax' state of mind."

Diomedes murmured back to Nestor, "Ajax is silent, but his silence is drinking up this applause!"

Ajax said, "If I go to him, I'll bash him in the face with my armored fist."

He began to swagger, and he continued to swagger.

"Oh, no, you shall not go to Achilles," Agamemnon said.

"And if Achilles acts proud in front of me, I'll fix his pride," Ajax said. "Let me go to him."

"Not for everything that we have spent on fighting this war," Ulysses said.

"Achilles is a paltry, insolent fellow!" Ajax said.

Nestor murmured, "How he describes himself!"

"Can't Achilles be sociable?" Ajax asked.

Ulysses murmured, "The raven chides blackness. The pot calls the kettle black."

"I'll make him bleed until his disposition improves," Ajax said.

Agamemnon murmured, "The man who wants to be the physician should instead be the patient."

"If all men were of my mind —" Ajax began.

Ulysses quietly finished Ajax' sentence, "— wit and intelligence would be out of fashion."

Ajax finished his sentence: "— he would not get away with his bad attitude. He would eat swords — and 's words — first. Shall pride get away with this and win and carry the day? Shall pride carry it?"

Nestor murmured, "If pride carries it, Ajax, you would carry half."

"He would have ten out of ten shares," Ulysses said. "He would carry all of it."

"I will knead Achilles with my fists," Ajax said. "I'll make him supple."

Nestor murmured to Ulysses, "Ajax is not yet thoroughly warm. Force him to eat and stuff himself with praises. Pour in, pour in, pour the praises into him — his ambition is still dry and withered."

Ulysses said to Agamemnon, "My lord, you feed too much on this discord and dissention. You are thinking too much about Achilles' bad behavior."

Nestor said, "Our noble general, do not do so. Don't think so much about Achilles."

Diomedes said, "You must prepare to fight without Achilles."

"Why, it is our talking so much about Achilles that makes him proud and does him harm," Ulysses said. "Here in our presence right now is a man — but I should not talk about him and praise him to his face; I will be silent."

"Why should you be silent?" Nestor asked. "He is not greedy for praise, as Achilles is."

"The whole world knows that he is as valiant and courageous as Achilles," Ulysses said.

"Achilles is a son of a bitch, a son of a whore," Ajax said. "He should not be treating us like this! I wish that he were a Trojan so I could fight him and kill him!"

"What a vice it would be in Ajax now —" Nestor said.

"— if he were proud —" Ulysses said.

"— or covetous of praise —" Diomedes said.

"Yes," Ulysses said, "or surly mannered —"

"— or aloof, or self-affected!" Diomedes said.

Ulysses said to Ajax, "Thank the Heavens, lord, that you have a sweet composure. Praise the father who begot you and the woman who breastfed you. May your tutor be famous, and your natural talents be three times famous, beyond the fame of all your erudition.

"But let he who disciplined your arms to fight — Mars, god of war — divide eternity in two, and give him half. As for your vigor, the famous athlete Milo, who carried a bull several yards and then killed it with a single blow and cooked and ate it all in one day, must yield his strongman title to muscular Ajax.

"I will not praise your wisdom, which is like a boundary, a fence, a shore that confines your spacious and ample accomplishments. Here in our presence is Nestor, who has learned much in his long life. He must be, he is, he cannot but be wise. But pardon me, father Nestor, when I say that if your days were as green and youthful as Ajax' days and if your brain were molded like Ajax' brain, then you would not be more eminent than him; instead, you would be like Ajax."

Ulysses said that he would not praise Ajax' wisdom, and he did not. Of course, Ulysses did not think that Ajax was wise. His words about Ajax' 'wisdom' were ambiguous. Ajax' wisdom *confined* Ajax' "spacious and ample accomplishments." Shouldn't wisdom *extend* one's spacious and ample accomplishments? And Ulysses said that Nestor is wise, but if Nestor were as young and inexperienced as Ajax and his brain were molded like Ajax' brain, then he would not be wiser than Ajax — he would be as stupid as Ajax.

Ajax asked Nestor, "Shall I call you father?"

"Yes, my good son," Nestor replied.

"Be ruled by him, Lord Ajax," Diomedes said. "Take whatever advice he gives you."

Ulysses said, "We ought not to tarry here. Achilles is like a deer that hides in a thicket. May it please our great general, Agamemnon, to call together all his armed forces. Fresh Kings have come to Troy. Tomorrow with all the might of our armed forces we must stand fast. And here before us is a lord: Ajax. If knights from east to west should come to Troy, and select their best, Ajax shall match the best."

"Let's go to council," Agamemnon said. "Let Achilles sleep: Light boats sail swift, though greater hulks draw deep. Light boats can be useful in war because they sail quickly; bigger ships sink deeper into the sea because of their weight, but that makes them slower."

CHAPTER 3

— 3.1 —

Pandarus and a servant talked together in a room in Priam's palace in Troy.

Pandarus said, "Friend, you! Please, let me have a word with you. Don't you follow the young Lord Paris?"

By "follow," Pandarus meant "serve"; that is, he was asking the man if he was one of Paris' servants.

Taking the word "follow" literally, the servant replied, "Yes, sir, when he goes before me."

"You depend upon him, I mean?" Pandarus said.

By "depend upon," Pandarus meant "wait upon." Servants were dependents on the Princes they served; they received room and board from the Princes.

The servant replied, "Sir, I do depend upon the Lord."

Now the servant had begun to use religious language. "The Lord" equals "God." But while the servant spoke of God, Pandarus spoke of social status. For him, "the lord" equals "the nobleman Paris."

"You depend upon a noble gentleman; I must necessarily praise him."

"Praise the Lord!" the servant said.

"You know who I am, don't you?" Pandarus asked.

"Yes, sir, but only superficially."

"Friend, know me better; I am the Lord Pandarus."

"I hope I shall know your honor better," the servant said.

The servant meant that he hoped he would learn that Pandarus had become a better and more honorable person, but Pandarus thought that the servant was saying that he wanted to be better acquainted with Pandarus.

"I do desire it," Pandarus said.

The servant said, "You are in the state of Grace."

A person in the state of Grace is a person who will go to Paradise when he or she dies, but Pandarus understood the word "Grace" to mean the way that a high-ranking person such as a Duke is addressed.

"'Grace'! I am not so, friend. 'Honor' and 'Lordship' are my titles," Pandarus said.

Music began to play.

"What music is this?" Pandarus asked.

The servant replied, "I do but partly know, sir. It is music in parts."

Music in parts had parts written for various musical instruments.

"Do you know the musicians?"

"Wholly, sir."

"Whom do they play to?"

"To the hearers, sir," the servant said.

"At whose pleasure, friend?"

"At mine, sir, and theirs who love music."

"I mean, command, friend," Pandarus said.

"Whom shall I command, sir?"

"Friend, we don't understand one another," Pandarus said. "I am too courtly and use too formal language, and you are too cunning and too willing to make puns. I am asking at whose command these musicians are playing — at whose request do these men play?"

"That's clear language and to the point, sir," the servant said. "Indeed, sir, the musicians are playing at the request of Paris, who is my lord, who is there in person; with him is the mortal Venus, the heart-blood of beauty, love's visible soul —"

"Whom do you mean? My niece Cressida?"

"No, sir. I mean Helen," the servant said. "Couldn't you tell by the way I described her?"

Venus was the immortal goddess of sexual passion, and Helen was the mortal Venus. Souls are invisible, but Helen was very visible and very beautiful.

"It should seem, fellow, that you have not seen the Lady Cressida," Pandarus said.

Cressida was also very visible and very beautiful.

Pandarus continued, "I have come from the Prince Troilus to speak with Paris. I will make a complimental assault upon Paris. I will batter him with compliments because my business seethes."

"Seethes" means "boils." Pandarus meant that his business with Paris was urgent.

"This is a sodden business!" the servant said. "There's a stewed phrase indeed!"

The servant was punning again. A sodden business was overboiled; overboiling makes food insipid. And the stews were brothels. By this time, many people, including the servant, Paris, and Helen, knew that Troilus and Cressida were in love — or at least infatuated — with each other and ready to hop into bed together. Pandarus was not willing to admit to himself that other people knew this.

Paris and Helen, accompanied by the musicians, entered the room.

Pandarus said, "Fair wishes to you, my lord, and to all this fair company! May fair desires, in all fair measure, fairly guide all of you! Especially you, fair Queen! May fair thoughts be your fair pillow!"

"Dear lord, you are full of fair words," Helen said.

"You speak your fair pleasure, sweet Queen," Pandarus replied. "Fair Prince, here is good broken music."

By "broken," he meant that the music was broken into different parts and arranged for different instruments.

"You have broken the music by interrupting it, friend," Paris said, "and, by my life, you shall make it whole again; you shall piece it out — augment it — with a piece of your own performance."

Helen said, "Pandarus is full of harmony."

"Truly, lady, no," he replied.

"Oh, sir —"

"My musical ability is amateurish," Pandarus said. "Truly, it is very amateurish."

"Well said, Pandarus!" Paris said. "Well, you say so in fits."

Paris was punning. "Fit" can mean "part of a song." But it can also mean "spasm." Pandarus was speaking in short bursts of words. Paris could also mean that Pandarus only sometimes stated that he was amateurish when it came to music.

"I have business with Paris, dear Queen," Pandarus said.

He then said to Paris, "My lord, will you grant me a word with you?"

Helen, who thought that Pandarus was making an excuse to get out of singing, said, "No, this shall not put us off. We'll hear you sing, certainly."

"Well, sweet Queen, you are joking with me," Pandarus said. "But, indeed, Paris, this is what I have to say: My dear lord and most esteemed friend, your brother Troilus —"

Helen interrupted, "My Lord Pandarus; honey-sweet lord —"

"In a moment, sweet Queen, in a moment," Pandarus said, then he started to complete the sentence that Helen had interrupted, "— commends himself most affectionately to you —"

Helen interrupted again, "You shall not cheat us out of our melody. If you do, then our melancholy will be upon your head!"

"Sweet Queen, sweet Queen!" Pandarus said. "You are a sweet Queen, truly."

"And to make a sweet lady sad is a sour offence," Helen said.

"No, that is not going to work," Pandarus said. "Your words shall not work, truly. No, I don't care for such words; no, no. And, Paris, Troilus wants you to make an excuse for him if King Priam calls for him at supper."

"My Lord Pandarus —" Helen said.

"What says my sweet Queen, my very, very sweet Queen?" Pandarus asked.

"What exploit is at hand?" Paris asked. "Where will Troilus eat tonight?"

Helen said to Pandarus, "No, but, my lord —"

"What says my sweet Queen?" Pandarus said. "My friend Paris will fall out with you if you keep interrupting me."

Helen said to Paris, "You must not know where Troilus eats tonight. Pandarus doesn't want you to know."

Paris replied, "I'll bet my life that Troilus will dine with my disposer Cressida."

A "disposer" is "one who commands." Paris was being gallant and saying that he obeyed Cressida's wishes.

"No, no, no such matter," Pandarus said. "You are wide of the mark. Come, your disposer is sick."

"Well, I'll make an excuse for Troilus' absence from the evening meal," Paris said.

By doing so, he was obeying Cressida's wishes; Cressida wished to spend time with Troilus.

"Good, my good lord," Pandarus said. "But why did you mention Cressida? No, your poor disposer's sick."

"I spy," Paris said.

He meant that his eyes were open and could see what was going on around him.

"You spy! What do you spy?" Pandarus blurted out of surprise.

To change the subject, he quickly said, "Come, give me a musical instrument. Now, sweet Queen."

"Why, this is kindly done," Helen said.

Realizing that Paris and Helen already knew about Troilus and Cressida, Pandarus said, "My niece is horribly in love with a thing you have, sweet Queen."

The word "thing" was slang for "penis." Helen had a lover; Cressida wanted a lover.

"She shall have it, my lord, if it is not my lord Paris," Helen said.

She meant that Cressida could have the thing, as long as it was not the "thing" that belonged to Paris.

"Paris'?" Pandarus said. "No, she'll have no part of him; Paris and Cressida are twain."

He meant that they were two separate beings and would not become one.

Helen said, "Falling in, after falling out, may make them three."

In other words, a man and a woman falling into bed together, after having quarreled and falling out of bed, could make the female pregnant. One meaning of "falling in" was "being reconciled," and one meaning of "falling out" was "quarreling." A penis could also "fall in" a vagina.

"Come, come, I'll hear no more of this," Pandarus said. "I'll sing you a song now."

"Yes, yes, now, please," Helen said. Flirtatiously, she said, "Truly, sweet lord, you have a fine forehead."

"You are joking with me," Pandarus said.

"Let your song be love. Sing this song: 'This Love will Undo Us All,'" Helen said. "Oh, Cupid, Cupid, Cupid!"

"Love!" Pandarus said. "Yes, that it shall, truly."

"Yes, good now," Paris said. He sang the first few lines of the song: "*Love, love, nothing but love.*"

"Indeed, that is the way the song begins," Pandarus said.

He sang the song:

"*Love, love, nothing but love, still more!*

"*For, oh, love's bow*

"*Shoots buck and doe.*

"The shaft confounds,

"Not what it wounds,

"But tickles always the sore."

The song stated that love affects males and females. The shaft of the arrow — symbol for penis — overwhelmed the wound — symbol for vagina. It did not distress the vagina; instead, it sexually tickled the vagina. By the way, the word "sore" also was used to refer to a four-year-old stag.

Pandarus continued to sing:

"These lovers cry, 'Oh! Oh!' They die!

"Yet that which seems the wound to kill,

"Does turn 'Oh! Oh!' to 'Ha! Ha! Ha!'

"So dying love lives still:

"'Oh! Oh!' a while, but then 'Ha! Ha! Ha!'

"'Oh! Oh!' groans become 'Ha! Ha! Ha!'

"Heigh-ho!"

The phrase "to die" was slang for "to have an orgasm." In the song, the penetration caused by the arrow — penis — hurt the wound, aka vagina, for a while, but then the pain of initial penetration turned into the pleasure of sexual orgasm.

"That is love, truly, to the very tip of the nose," Helen said.

A nose is something that prominently protrudes, much like a male part used in sex.

Paris said to Helen, "Love, Pandarus eats nothing but doves — the birds of Venus — and that breeds hot blood, and hot blood begets hot thoughts, and hot thoughts beget hot deeds, and hot deeds are love."

"Is this the generation — the genealogy — of love? Is this how love is created?" Pandarus asked. "Hot blood, hot thoughts, and hot deeds? Why, they are vipers: Is love a generation of vipers?"

The offspring of vipers are cruel. If love were to be a generation — an offspring — of vipers, then love would be cruel. People in this culture incorrectly believed that vipers were born by gnawing their way out of the body of their mother.

This is Matthew 3:7 in the 1599 Geneva Bible: *"Now when he saw many of the Pharisees, and of the Sadducees come to his baptism, he said unto them, O generation of vipers, who hath forewarned you to flee from the anger to come?"*

This is Matthew 12:34 in the 1599 Geneva Bible: "*O generations of vipers, how can you speak good things, when ye are evil? For of the abundance of the heart the mouth speaketh.*"

Pandarus asked Paris, "Sweet lord, who's on the battlefield today?"

Paris replied, "Hector, Deiphobus, Helenus, Antenor, and all the gallant nobility of Troy. I would have gladly armed myself and fought today, but my Nell — my Helen — would not allow me to do so. How does it happen that my brother Troilus did not go to the battlefield today?"

Helen said, "He is pouting at something. You know everything about Troilus, Lord Pandarus."

"Not I, honey-sweet Queen," Pandarus replied. "I long to hear how our soldiers fared today."

He said to Paris, "You'll remember to make an excuse at the evening meal tonight for your brother Troilus?"

"Yes, exactly as you wish," Paris replied.

"Farewell, sweet Queen," Pandarus said.

"Give my best wishes to your niece," Helen said.

"I will, sweet Queen," Pandarus said.

He exited.

A military trumpet sounded.

"They're returning from the battlefield," Paris said. "Let us go to Priam's hall to greet the warriors. Sweet Helen, I must persuade you to help unarm our Hector. His buckles, which can be unyielding, shall obey the touch of your white enchanting fingers more than they do the steel edge of a Greek sword or the force of Greek muscles. You shall do more than all the Greek Kings who rule islands can do — disarm great Hector."

"It will make us proud to be his servant, Paris," Helen said, using the royal plural. "Yes, what he shall receive of us in duty will give us more honor than we receive because of our beauty — the honor we receive by serving Hector will outshine ourself."

"Sweetheart, above thought I love you," Paris said.

Paris did love her more than thought. If he had taken thought, he might have come to believe that Helen was not worth the death of so many Trojans and Greeks and the destruction of Troy. Perhaps in some cases love really is the offspring of vipers.

In his garden, Pandarus spoke to Troilus' servant, a young boy.

"Hello!" Pandarus said to the servant. "Where's your master? At my niece Cressida's?"

"No, sir; he is waiting for you to lead him there."

Pandarus said, "Oh, here he comes."

Troilus entered the garden.

Pandarus said, "Hello. How are you now?"

He said to Troilus' servant, "You may leave."

The servant exited.

Pandarus asked Troilus, "Have you seen my niece?"

"No, Pandarus. I stalk about her door, like a soul who has newly arrived at the banks of the River Styx and who is waiting for waftage — transport by boat across the river — by Charon, the ferryman to the Land of the Dead. Oh, be my Charon, and give me swift transport to those Elysian Fields, the abode of the good souls in Hades. In the Elysian Fields, I may wallow in the lily-beds that are promised for the good souls. Oh, gentle Pandarus, from Cupid's shoulder pluck his colorful wings and use them to fly with me to Cressida! Help me to cross the threshold of your niece's door!"

"Walk here in the garden," Pandarus said. "I'll bring her to you quickly."

He exited.

Alone, Troilus said to himself, "I am giddy and dizzy; anticipation whirls me round. The imaginary relish is so sweet that it enchants my sense. What will the reality be when the salivating palate tastes for real love's thrice purified nectar? I am afraid that the result will be death, swooning destruction, or some joy too fine, too subtle-potent and powerfully refined and tuned too sharp in sweetness, for the capacity of my ruder powers. I very much fear this; and I also fear that I shall lose distinction in my joys, as does an army when the soldiers charge in mass to pursue and kill the fleeing enemy."

"Distinction" means "the ability to differentiate." If Troilus and Cressida were to have sex, two would become one. When they orgasmed, they would "die." An army pursuing fleeing enemies can kill indiscriminately — kill quickly and without discriminating soldiers of high rank from soldiers of low rank.

Pandarus returned and said, "She's getting ready; she'll come here soon. You must keep your wits about you. She blushes very much, and she breathes quickly and shallowly, as if a ghost had frightened her. I'll bring her to you. She is the prettiest villain. She breathes as quickly and shallowly as a newly taken sparrow."

Newly captured birds are very frightened, and because of their fright they breathe quickly and shallowly.

Pandarus exited.

Alone, Troilus said to himself, "Exactly such a passion embraces my bosom. My heart beats faster than a feverish pulse, and I am losing the use of all my senses, as if I were a lowly born person unexpectedly seeing his King looking at him."

Pandarus returned, leading Cressida.

Pandarus said to her, "Come, come, what need do you have to blush? Shame's a baby."

Pandarus meant that shame was something little; however, in this culture a child of shame was a baby born out of wedlock.

He said to Troilus, "Here she is now. Now swear the oaths to her that you have sworn to me."

Cressida moved as if she were going to leave the garden. Pandarus grabbed her arm and said, "What, are you gone again? You must be watched before you are made tame, must you? Come on, come on; if you draw backward, we'll put you in harness."

When Pandarus referred to Cressida, he used terms that likened her to a bird or other animal. He had already likened her to a newly caught sparrow. When he mentioned watching her until she be made tame, he was referring to a method of taming a hawk: breaking its will by not allowing it to sleep. And he referred to her as a skittish horse that needed to be harnessed to a cart.

Pandarus said to Troilus, "Why don't you speak to her?"

Pandarus then said to Cressida, who was wearing a veil, "Come, draw this curtain, and let's see your picture."

In this culture, a curtain was hung before a painting. To see the painting, one had to draw the curtain. To see Cressida's face, her veil had to be removed.

Pandarus removed Cressida's veil and said, "Pity the day; how loath you are to offend daylight! If it were dark, you would close sooner."

Night had not yet fallen. Pandarus was saying that he felt sorry for the daylight, in the presence of which Cressida was unwilling to offend — to stumble morally. But if it were dark, she would close the distance between herself and Troilus and they would offend together.

Troilus moved to Cressida, and they kissed.

Pandarus said to Troilus, "Good, good. Rub on, and kiss the mistress."

Pandarus' language referred to the game of bowls, in which "to rub" is "to negotiate an obstacle" and "to kiss the mistress" is "to gently touch the little ball aimed at in the game of bowling." Of course, Pandarus used the phrase "to rub" to mean "to create sexual friction by rubbing against Cressida" and "to kiss the mistress" to mean "to kiss Cressida."

Pandarus said, "Great! A kiss in fee-farm!"

He was referring to a long kiss. "Fee-farm" meant "in perpetuity." It is a legal term referring to land granted in perpetuity with a permanently fixed rent.

Pandarus said to Troilus, "Build there, carpenter; the air is sweet."

Where the air is sweet is a good place to build a structure. In this case, Pandarus wanted Troilus to build a six-inch structure.

Pandarus said to both Troilus and Cressida, "You shall fight your hearts out before I part you. The falcon as the tercel, for all the ducks in the river. Go to it. Go to it."

The kind of "fight" that Pandarus referred to involved a kind of wrestling in bed. A falcon is a female hawk; a tercel is a male hawk. Pandarus was saying that when it comes to the act of sex, males and females are alike — ready and eager to get down to it. He would bet everything — all the ducks in the river — that this is true.

Troilus said to Cressida, "You have bereft me of all words, lady."

Pandarus said to Troilus, "Words pay no debts, give her deeds, but she'll bereave — deprive — you of the deeds, too, if she calls your activity into question."

The "deeds" Pandarus referred to were sexual deeds, or acts, but "deeds" also means "legal documents." In this culture, "to pay one's debts" was slang for "to have sex." Sex is something a wife owes a husband, and it is something a husband owes a wife. "Activity" means "vigorous action," or "virility." If Cressida were to call into question — doubt — Troilus' virility, or ability to have sex with her, she would deprive him of the opportunity to have sex with her. However, if calling his virality into question involved testing his virality, she would leave him sexually exhausted and unable to perform any longer.

Troilus and Cressida kissed again.

Pandarus added, "What, billing again? Here's 'In witness whereof the parties interchangeably.'"

"Billing" meant both "kissing" and "drawing up a legal document."

Legal contracts used language such as "In witness whereof the parties interchangeably" in which "interchangeably" meant "reciprocally." One kind of legal contract is a marriage. In this culture, the man and woman could hold hands in front of witnesses and pledge themselves to each other in a prelude to a legal marriage.

Pandarus said, "Come in, come in. I'll go get a fire."

He left to start a fire in the bedroom where he hoped Troilus and Cressida would spend the night together.

"Will you walk into my house, my lord?" Cressida said to Troilus.

In this culture, wives called their husband "lord."

"Oh, Cressida, how often have I wished to do that!"

"Wished, my lord! May the gods grant — oh, my lord!"

"What should the gods grant?" Troilus asked. "What is the reason for this pretty interruption? What too-curious — hidden — dreg does my sweet lady see in the fountain of our love?"

"I see more dregs than water, if my fears have eyes," Cressida replied.

"Fears make Devils of the high order of Angels known as the Cherubim," Troilus replied. "Fears never see truly."

"Blind fear that is led by seeing reason finds safer footing than blind reason that stumbles without fear," Cressida said. "Seeing reason leads to prudence, while blind reason leads to sin. Fearing the worst often cures the worse. If we fear, we can often avoid the worst."

"Oh, let my lady apprehend no fear," Troilus said. "In all Cupid's pageant, no monster appears."

In this culture, one meaning of "pageant" is "a performance intended to trick." Another meaning is "a theatrical play." Troilus wanted to take Cressida to bed, and so he was minimizing the monsters that can participate in plays featuring Cupid, aka love. Romantic love has its pleasures, but it can also have its pains. Infidelity can greatly hurt one who loves.

"Nor nothing monstrous either?" Cressida asked.

"Nothing, but our undertakings — the things we promise to do," Troilus replied. "When we vow to weep seas, live in fire, eat rocks, tame tigers, we think it harder for our female loved one to devise difficult enough tasks than for us to undergo any difficulty imposed. The monstruosity in love, lady, is that the will is infinite and the execution is confined, and that the desire is boundless and the act is a slave to limit."

This is true in more ways than one. The desire to have sex is boundless, but the act of sex lasts only a short time. A lover can promise to be faithful — and mean it — but not live up to the promise.

Knowing this, Cressida said, "They say all lovers swear more performance than they are capable of and continue to keep in reserve an ability that they never perform, vowing more than the perfection of ten and discharging less than the tenth part of one. Lovers who have the voice of lions and the act of hares, are they not monsters?"

"Do such lovers exist?" Troilus asked. Using the royal plural, he said, "We are not like them. Praise us according to how we act when put to the test, acknowledge us as we show ourself to be; our head shall go bare until merit crown it. No perfection expected to be possessed in the future shall have any praise in the present. We will not name desert before its birth, and, being born, its title of honor shall be humble. Judge me by my actions.

"You know the proverb 'Where many words are, the truth goes by,' so let me say a few words about my fair faith. Troilus shall act in such a way to Cressida as to make the worst that envy and malice can say about him is to mock him for his faithfulness to you. The truest speech of truth itself shall not be truer than the speech of Troilus."

"Will you walk into my house, my lord?" Cressida asked Troilus.

Pandarus returned.

"What, blushing still?" he said. "Haven't you two finished talking yet?"

"Well, uncle," Cressida said, "whatever folly I commit, I dedicate to you."

"I thank you for that," Pandarus said. "If Troilus gets you pregnant with a boy, you'll give him to me."

Pandarus was giving Troilus credit for masculinity: If Troilus were to get Cressida pregnant, it would be with a boy.

Pandarus continued, "Be true to Troilus; if he flinches and sneaks away, rebuke me for it."

Of course, Pandarus knew that Troilus would not flinch and sneak away.

"You know now your hostages: your uncle's word and my firm faith," Troilus said.

Hostages were guarantees of good conduct. In war, an important person might enter an enemy camp to parley. Before the important person entered the camp, an important enemy would be sent to the important person's camp to be a hostage. If anything happened to the important person, the important hostage would be killed.

"I'll give my word for her, too, as well as for you," Pandarus said. "Our kindred, although they have to be wooed for a long time, are faithful once they are won. They are burs, I can tell you; they'll stick where they are thrown."

"Boldness comes to me now, and brings me courage," Cressida said. "Prince Troilus, I have loved you night and day for many weary months."

"Why was my Cressida then so hard to win?" Troilus asked.

"I seemed hard to win," she replied, "but I was won, my lord, with the first glance that ever — pardon me — if I confess much, you will play the tyrant and lord it over me. I love you now, but I did not love you, until now, so much but I could master it. Actually, I lie. My thoughts were like unbridled, uncontrolled children, grown too headstrong for their mother to manage. See, my thoughts and I are fools! Why have I blabbed? Who shall be true to us and keep our secrets, when we cannot keep our own secrets? But, although I very much loved you, I did not woo you. And yet, truly, I wished that I had a man, or that we women had men's privilege of speaking and confessing our love first. Sweetheart, tell me to hold my tongue because in this rapture of emotion I shall surely say something that I shall repent saying. I see that your silence, which is cunning in its lack of speech, from my weakness draws the heart of speech! Stop me from speaking!"

"I shall, albeit sweet music comes from your mouth," Troilus said, kissing her.

"This is indeed a pretty sight," Pandarus said.

"My lord, I ask you to pardon me," Cressida said to Troilus. "I did not intend to beg for a kiss. I am ashamed. Oh, Heavens! What have I done? For this time I will take my leave, my lord."

"You are leaving, sweet Cressida!" Troilus said.

"Leave!" Pandarus said. "If you take leave until tomorrow morning —"

"Please," Cressida said. "Don't talk about that."

"What offends you, lady?" Troilus asked.

"Sir, my own company."

"You cannot shun yourself."

"Let me go and try," Cressida replied. "I have a kind of self that stays with you, but it is an unnatural self that will leave itself in order to be another's fool. I want to leave. Where is my good sense? I don't know what I am saying."

"People who speak so wisely know well what they are speaking," Troilus said.

The part of Cressida's speech that Troilus thought was wise was the part about the self that stayed with him.

Cressida replied, "Perhaps, my lord, I am showing more cunning than love, and fell so outspokenly into a frank confession in order to fish for your thoughts, but you are too wise to reveal your thoughts, or in other words you do not love, for to be wise and to love exceeds the power of man; only the gods above can be both wise and in love."

"Oh, I wish that I thought it could be in a woman — as, if it can, I will presume that it could be in you — to feed forever her lamp and the flames of love, to keep her faithfulness in as fit and youthful a condition as it was when it was plighted with the result that it will outlive outward beauty, with a mind that renews love swifter than passion decays! I also wish that I could be persuaded that my integrity and faithfulness to you might be equaled by your own integrity and faithfulness to me. Let us both have an equal amount of pure love winnowed from the chaff. How elated would I then be! But unfortunately I am as true as the simplicity of truth and I am more innocent than the infancy of truth. I am more innocent than infants, and I am more innocent than Adam before the fall."

"When it comes to faithfulness, I'll war — compete — with you," Cressida said.

"Oh, this is a virtuous fight, when right wars with right over who shall be most right!" Troilus said. "Faithful lovers shall in the world of the future confirm their faithfulness by comparing it with that of Troilus. When their rhyming love poems, full of declarations of love, of oaths and big comparisons, lack similes, when faithfulness is described with tired comparisons — as faithful as steel, as faithful as plants are to the Moon, as faithful as the Sun is to the day, as faithful as the turtledove is to her mate, as faithful as iron is attracted to a magnet, as faithful as the Earth is to its center — after all these comparisons of faithfulness are made, then faithfulness' authentic author shall be cited. 'As faithful as Troilus' shall crown the verse, and sanctify the verses."

"May you prove to be a prophet!" Cressida said. "If I am unfaithful to you, or swerve a hair from being true to you, then when time is old and has forgotten itself, when drops of rain have worn down the stones of Troy, and blind oblivion has swallowed entire cities up, and mighty states are worn away by time into dusty nothing and leave no trace of themselves, yet let memory, from unfaithfulness to unfaithfulness, among unfaithful maidens in love, upbraid my unfaithfulness! When they've said 'as false as air, as false as water, wind, or sandy earth, as false as fox to lamb, as false as wolf to heifer's calf, as false as panther to the deer, or as false as evil stepmother to her stepson,' then let them say to stick the heart of unfaithfulness, 'as unfaithful as Cressida.'"

How can air, water, wind, and sandy earth be false, aka unfaithful? The ancient Roman poet Catullus once wrote, "*Sed mulier cupido quod dicit amanti / in vento et rapida scribere oportet aqua.*" Translated into English: "But the words a woman says to a passionate lover / ought to be written on wind and running water." If the words were to be written on air or sandy earth, they would not last long.

Pandarus said, "All right, this is a bargain you two have made. Seal it, seal it. I'll be the witness. In this hand I hold Troilus' hand, and in this hand I hold my niece's hand. If ever you prove false — unfaithful — one to the other, since I have taken such pains to bring you together, let all pitiful goers-between be called until the world's end after my name — call them all Panders. Let all faithful men be Troiluses, all unfaithful women Cressidas, and all brokers-between Panders! Say, 'Amen.'"

Troilus said, "Amen."

Cressida said, "Amen."

Pandarus said, "Amen. Now I will take you to a chamber with a bed; because the bed shall not speak of your pretty encounters, press it to death. Go into the bedroom now!"

In the act of lovemaking, Troilus' weight would be on Cressida, and the weight of both would press on the bed. In this culture, "to die" meant "to have an orgasm" and so Pandarus wanted Troilus and Cressida to press the bed until they both had orgasms. But Pandarus' words also referred to an act of torture or capital punishment. A prisoner could be pressed to death. More and more weight would be piled on his chest until his torturers heard the words they wanted the prisoner to say, or until the prisoner's chest was crushed and he died.

Pressing was done when a prisoner would refuse to stand trial for an offense. Sometimes, a prisoner would refuse to plead guilty or not guilty in a trial because if they were found guilty their property would be forfeited to the state, which often meant that the prisoners' loved ones would be destitute. Rather than risking being found guilty, sentenced to death, and having his property forfeited to the state, thereby making his loved ones destitute, the prisoner would choose to die by being pressed to death. This is what Giles Corey chose in the Salem Witch Trials of 1692 in Salem, Massachusetts.

Troilus and Cressida went inside the house and into the bedroom, and Pandarus said to you, the reader, "And may Cupid grant all tongue-tied virgins — male or female — reading this a bed, a bedchamber, and a Pander to provide all this gear!"

In all the conversation among Troilus, Cressida, and Pandarus, no one mentioned legal marriage.

— 3.3 —

Agamemnon, Ulysses, Diomedes, Nestor, Ajax, Menelaus, and Calchas met in the Greek camp near Achilles' tent. Calchas was a Trojan — Cressida's father. He was a prophet who knew that Troy would be defeated in the war and who had joined the Greeks.

Calchas said, "Now, Princes, for the service I have done you, the opportunity provided to me at this time prompts me to call aloud for recompense. May you remember that, through the prophetic foresight I have, I know that Troy will lose the war. Therefore, I have abandoned Troy, left my possessions, incurred a traitor's name for myself, left certain and possessed advantages, and exposed myself to doubtful fortunes, separating myself from all that time, acquaintance, custom, and social rank made habitual and most familiar to my nature, and here, to do you service, I am become like a new person entering into the world, a foreigner, unacquainted with anyone. I ask you, as a foretaste of what will be in the future, to give me now a little benefit, out of those many benefits that you have promised to me, which, you say, will come to me in the future."

"What would you ask of us, Trojan?" Agamemnon asked. "Make your demand."

"You have a Trojan prisoner, named Antenor, who was captured yesterday," Calchas said. "Troy regards him as very valuable. Often have you — and often have you received my thanks because of it — desired my Cressida in exchange for an important Trojan held prisoner by you, but Troy has always refused to make the exchange. However, this Antenor, I know, is such a tuning peg in the Trojans' affairs that their negotiations all must go out of tune when the Trojans lack his managerial skills. Antenor is the key to the harmonious management of Trojan affairs, and therefore the Trojans will almost give us a Prince of blood, a son of Priam, in exchange for him. Let Antenor be sent, great Princes, in exchange for my daughter, and her presence shall quite pay for all the service I have done in most willingly endured pain."

"Let Diomedes bear Antenor to Troy, and bring Cressida to us here," Agamemnon said. "Calchas shall have what he requests of us. Good Diomedes,

73

get everything you need for this exchange. Also take word to Troy that Hector will tomorrow be answered in his challenge: Ajax is ready."

"This shall I undertake," Diomedes said, "and it is a burden that I am proud to bear."

Diomedes and Calchas exited.

Achilles and Patroclus came out of their tent and stood there. They could see the other Greeks, but they could not hear them.

Ulysses said, "Achilles is standing in the entrance of his tent. May it please our general, Agamemnon, to pass like a stranger by him, as if Achilles were forgotten, and for all the Princes to lay negligent and casual regard upon him. We ought not to pay any special attention to Achilles, although we did in the past when he fought well for us. I will bring up the rear. It is likely that Achilles will ask me why such disapproving eyes are bent on him. If he does ask me, I will use your derision as medicine for him. Your disapproval will injure his pride, he will ask me why you disapprove, and I will give him medicine that, because he asked for it, he desires to drink. This may turn out well. Pride has no other mirror to show itself but pride because supple knees feed arrogance and are the proud man's fees. If Achilles sees us acting proud, he may realize how proudly he has been acting. If we show courtesy to him, he will become even more arrogant and will think that we are only paying him the respect that is due him."

"We'll execute your plan, and put on an appearance of coldness and disapproval as we pass by Achilles," Agamemnon said. "Each lord here, do this. Either don't speak to and greet Achilles, or if you do, do it disdainfully, which shall shake him more than if we don't even look at him. I will lead the way."

The Greeks walked toward Achilles' tent, intending — all but Ulysses — to pass by it.

Achilles said, "Is the general, Agamemnon, coming here to speak with me? You know my mind, I'll fight no more against Troy."

Agamemnon asked Nestor, "What did Achilles say? Does he want anything?"

Nestor asked Achilles, "Do you, my lord, have anything to say to Agamemnon?"

"No," Achilles replied.

Nestor said to Agamemnon, "He wants nothing, my lord."

"Very good," Agamemnon said.

Agamemnon and Nestor exited.

Seeing Menelaus, Achilles said, "Good day. Good day."

Menelaus replied, "How are you? How are you?"

Menelaus exited.

Achilles to Patroclus, "Does the cuckold scorn me?"

Ajax said, "How are you now, Patroclus?"

"Good morning, Ajax," Achilles said.

"What?" Ajax said.

"Good morning."

"Yes, and it will be a good next day, too."

Ajax exited.

"Why are these fellows acting like this?" Achilles said. "Don't they know that I am Achilles?"

Patroclus said, "They pass by you as if you were a stranger. They used to bend their knee to you and to send their smiles before themselves to you, Achilles. They used to come to you as humbly as they used to approach holy altars."

"Have I become poor recently?" Achilles said. "It is certain that a great man, once fallen out with fortune, and therefore out of luck, must fall out with men, too. What the man whose fortunes have declined is, he shall as soon read in the eyes of other people as feel in his own fall, for men, like butterflies, don't show their powdered wings except to the summer. No man receives any honor for simply being a man; he receives honor for those honors that are outside him, such as social rank, riches, and favor. These are prizes of accident as often as they are prizes of merit. When these prizes fall, as is likely they will since they are slippery supports, the respect that leaned on them will be as slippery, too. One will fall and pull down another, and both of them will die in the fall. But it is not so with me: Fortune and I are friends. I still enjoy at the highest point all that I ever did possess, with the exception of these men's looks, which once were respectful but now are not. These men, I think, have discovered something in me that is not worth such rich beholding as they have often previously given to me. Here is Ulysses; I'll interrupt his reading."

"How are you, Ulysses?" Achilles said.

Closing the book he had been looking at, Ulysses said, "Hello, great Thetis' son!"

"What are you reading?"

Ulysses replied, "A strange fellow here writes, 'That man, however dearly gifted by nature, however much he possesses in material objects, however blessed he is either outwardly or inwardly, cannot boast about having that which he has, and does not feel what he owns, except by reflection, as when his virtues shining upon others heat them and they return that heat again to the first giver.'"

A person cannot boast about great wealth unless there are other people to whom that person can boast; a person cannot know that he possesses a virtue such as courage unless that person exhibits courage to witnesses who then acknowledge that that person is courageous.

"This is not strange, Ulysses," Achilles said. "A beautiful person does not know the beauty that is borne here in the face; the beauty presents itself to the eyes of other people. Also, the eye itself, sight being the purest of senses, does not behold itself; an eye cannot leave itself and turn around and look at itself. However, one eye opposed to another can salute each other with each other's form; I can look at your eye, and you can look at my eye. Sight cannot look at itself until it has traveled and is mirrored in a place where it may see itself; we can see our eyes in a mirror or on the surface of calm water. This is not strange at all."

"I do not have difficulty accepting the hypothesis — it is well known — but I have difficulty accepting the author's conclusion," Ulysses said. "The author, in his detailed argument, expressly proves that no man is the lord of anything, though in and of himself he possesses many good qualities, until he communicates his good qualities to other people. Nor does the man himself know that he possesses the good qualities until he beholds them formed in the applause of those people to whom they're extended. These people, like an arch, echo the voice again, or, like a gate of steel facing the Sun, receive and render back his figure and his heat. In other words, the man displays the good qualities in front of and for the benefit of other people, they acknowledge the good qualities with applause, and the man knows for sure that he has the good qualities."

Ulysses had said that he had difficulty accepting the author's conclusion. His difficulty concerned reputation because a man could get an undeserved reputation for possessing qualities he did not actually possess; however, it is possible for a man to prove by his actions that he definitely possesses certain qualities. Ulysses wanted Achilles to show his good qualities; one way for Achilles to display his fighting ability was to battle the Trojans.

Ulysses continued, "I was much interested by what the author said, and I immediately thought of the unknown Ajax here. Heavens, what a man is there! A veritable horse, who has he knows not what. Nature, what things there are that are most despicable in reputation and yet are precious in use!

"And what things again are most dear in esteem and yet are poor in worth!

"Now we shall see tomorrow — an act that true chance throws upon him — Ajax renowned."

Ulysses was referring to the duel that Ajax would fight with Hector the next day. Supposedly, chance — a lottery — had chosen Hector's opponent, but Ulysses had rigged the lottery so that Ajax would be chosen.

He continued, "Oh, Heavens, what some men do, while some men leave undone! How some men creep into fickle Fortune's hall, while others act like idiots in her eyes! Some people pursue Fortune's gifts, while others neglect Fortune's gifts. Some people move slowly and carefully to get Fortune's gifts, while others showily act like idiots as they ignore Fortune's gifts. How one man eats into another's pride, while pride is fasting in his wantonness!"

Achilles was the man who was leaving things undone. He was not fighting on the battlefield. Ajax and Hector, however, were dueling the next day. Achilles was the man who was neglecting the gifts that Lady Fortune had given to him, while Ajax was the man approaching Lady Fortune and asking her for gifts. Achilles was the proud man who was fasting; he was not doing the things that would add to his reputation. Ajax was doing those things — dueling with Hector and fighting on the battlefield — and therefore he was eating and acquiring the pride that should have been Achilles'.

Part of Ulysses' strategy to get Achilles to obey Agamemnon and return to fighting was to make him feel that Ajax was receiving the honor that Achilles should earn, and that Ajax did not deserve that honor.

Ulysses continued, "To see these Greek lords! Why, even already they clap the blundering Ajax on the shoulder, as if his foot were on brave Hector's breast and the citizens of great Troy were shrieking at Hector's death."

"I believe it," Achilles said, "for the Greek lords passed by me the way that misers pass by beggars; they gave to me neither respectful words or looks. Have my deeds been forgotten?"

Ulysses replied, "Time has, my lord, a bag on his back in which he puts good deeds that are destined for oblivion, which is a huge monster of ingratitude. Things that ought to be remembered are instead forgotten. Those good deeds are past good deeds; they are devoured as fast as they are made, and they are forgotten as soon as they are done. Perseverance, my dear lord, keeps honor bright. To continue to be honored and respected, you must continue to do deeds that bring you honor and respect. If you stop doing those deeds, you become quite out of fashion; you are like a rusty coat of armor hanging on the wall — a monument that mocks past deeds.

"Take the quickest way, for honor travels in a cramped passage so narrow that only one can walk abreast at a time. Keep then to the path, for emulation and ambitious rivalry have a thousand sons that in single file pursue you. If you give way, or deviate from the direct and straight path, then they will all rush by you like a tide flooding in and leave you behind. Or if you give way, or deviate from the direct and straight path, then like a gallant horse fallen in the front line, you will lie there and serve as pavement for the abject and despicable soldiers in the rear; you will be run over and trampled on.

"Then what deeds people do in the present, although those deeds are less than your past deeds, must overtop and surpass your deeds because time is like a fashionable host who slightly shakes hands with his parting guest, and with his arms outstretched, as if he would fly, embraces the newcomer. Welcome always smiles, and farewell goes out sighing.

"Oh, let not virtue seek remuneration for the thing it was because beauty, wit and intelligence, high birth, vigor of body, desert in service, love, friendship, and charity are all subject to envious and slanderous time.

"One trait of human nature makes everyone in the whole world kin — all with one consent praise new and gaudy toys, although they are made and molded of old things, and they give more praise to dust that is sprinkled with a little gold than they give to gold that is sprinkled with a little dust. The present eye praises the present object; what gets praised is what is in front of people's eyes.

"Then marvel not, you great and complete man, that all the Greeks begin to worship Ajax since things in motion sooner catch the eye than what does not stir or move. The cry of approval went once to you, and still it might, and yet it may again, if you would not entomb yourself alive and encase your reputation in your tent. Your glorious deeds, which you displayed in the fields of battle recently, made the envious gods go to war themselves and even drove great Mars to take sides in the war."

Mars supported the Trojans and even occasionally fought in battles on their side.

"I have strong reasons for my isolation," Achilles said.

"But the reasons against your isolation are more potent and heroic," Ulysses said, adding, "It is known, Achilles, that you are in love with one of Priam's daughters."

"Really!" Achilles said. "It is known!"

"Is that a surprise?" Ulysses asked. "The providential foresight that's in a watchful government knows almost every grain of gold belonging to the god of the underworld, Pluto. It finds the bottom in the incomprehensible deeps of the sea, it keeps pace with thought and it almost, like the gods, unveils thoughts as soon as they are born and placed in their dumb cradles."

In other words, the leaders of the Greek army had a very good spy network.

Ulysses continued, "The heart of the government is a mystery, a secret — which open discussion dares never meddle with. It has an operation more divine than breath and speech or pen and writing can give expression to.

"All the commerce and interaction that you have had with Troy we know about as well as you do, my lord, and it would be more fitting for Achilles to throw down Hector in the dust than Hector's sister Polyxena on a bed.

"But it must grieve your son, the young Pyrrhus Neoptolemus, who is now at home in Greece, when rumor shall in our islands sound her trumpet, and all the Greek girls shall dance and sing, 'Great Hector's sister did Achilles win, but our great Ajax bravely beat down him.'"

The word "him" was ambiguous and referred to both Hector and Achilles. Ajax beat down Hector by defeating him in battle or a duel, and Ajax beat down Achilles by acquiring a greater reputation in war than Achilles did.

Ulysses concluded, "Farewell, my lord. I speak as your friend when I say that the fool slides over the ice that you should break."

The fool is Ajax, who skates over ice and does not break it. Achilles, in contrast, would break the ice. He is the one who would make a good beginning in a difficult enterprise. He would be like a big ship that goes first and breaks the ice so that other, smaller ships can follow in his wake. He is the warrior who would break the line of the opposing warriors.

Ulysses exited, leaving Achilles with things to think about.

Patroclus said, "To this effect, Achilles, have I appealed to you. A woman who is impudent and mannish is not more loathed than an effeminate man during a time in which action is required. The woman here is Polyxena, who is impudent and like a man because she loves a warrior who is an enemy to her city and family. The man is me, who stands condemned because the other Greek warriors think my little stomach for the war and your great friendship for me restrains you and keeps you away from the war. Sweet Achilles, rouse yourself; and the weak, wanton Cupid shall from your neck unloose his amorous fold, and, like a dew-drop from the lion's mane, Cupid shall be shook into the air. Give up Polyxena, and go to war."

"Shall Ajax fight with Hector?" Achilles asked.

"Yes, and perhaps he will receive much honor by dueling him," Patroclus said.

"I see that my reputation is at stake," Achilles said. "My fame is seriously and deeply wounded."

"Oh, then, beware," Patroclus said. "Wounds that men give themselves heal badly. Neglecting to do what is necessary gives a blank check to danger, and danger, like a fever, deceitfully infects us even when we sit idly in the Sun."

In this culture, people believed that sitting in the sunshine in March could give one a fever.

"Go call the Fool Thersites here, sweet Patroclus," Achilles said. "I'll send the Fool to Ajax and ask him to invite the Trojan lords here to see us unarmed after the combat. I have a woman's longing, an appetite that I am sick with, to see great Hector in his clothing of peace rather than in his armor, to talk with him and to wholly see his face rather than to see only the little that is visible when he wears a helmet."

Thersites came walking over to them.

Seeing Thersites, Achilles said, "A labor saved!"

"A wonder!" Thersites said.

"What?" Achilles asked.

"Ajax goes up and down the field, asking for himself," Thersites said.

If Ajax were asking for himself, he was asking for a jakes — a toilet.

"How so?" Achilles asked.

"He must fight a duel tomorrow with Hector, and he is so prophetically proud of an heroic cudgeling that he raves in saying nothing," Thersites said.

Ajax was confident that he would defeat Hector the following day. Thersites was equally confident that Hector would defeat Ajax.

"How can that be?" Achilles asked.

"Why, Ajax stalks up and down like a peacock, a symbol of pride — a stride and a stop. He ruminates like a hostess who has no arithmetic but her brain to add up and set down the customers' bill. He bites his lip with a shrewd regard, attempting to look intelligent, as who should say, 'There is intelligence in this head, as all would know if it would get out,' and so there is, but the intelligence in his head lies as coldly in him as fire in a piece of flint, which will not show itself without knocking the flint against metal. To get to Ajax' intelligence, you will have to break his head.

"Ajax is undone — ruined — forever because if Hector does not break Ajax' neck in the duel, Ajax will break his own neck in vainglory, aka excessive vanity.

"Ajax doesn't know me. I said, 'Good morning, Ajax,' and he replied, 'Thanks, Agamemnon.' What do you think of this man who mistakes me for the general? He's grown and become a very land-fish — a fish on land — without knowledge of language and unable to speak, aka a monster.

"A plague on opinion and reputation! A man may wear it on both sides, like a reversible leather jacket."

Opinion and reputation are two sides of the same coin, or of the two sides — inside and outside — of a reversible leather jacket. Opinion is inside a man; it is what he thinks about himself. Reputation is outside a man; it is what other people say about him. Both opinion and reputation can ruin a man. Ulysses had wanted to build up Ajax' pride in order to bring Achilles' pride down, but Ajax was well on his way to becoming as proud as Achilles.

"You must be my ambassador to Ajax, Thersites," Achilles said.

"Who, I?" Thersites replied. "Why, he'll answer nobody; he practices not answering. Speaking is for beggars; he wears his tongue in his arms — he lets his fighting do his speaking for him. I will pretend to be him: Let Patroclus ask me questions as if I were Ajax, and you shall see a play starring Ajax."

"Do it, Patroclus," Achilles said. "Tell him that I humbly desire the valiant Ajax to invite the most valorous Hector to come unarmed to my tent, and to procure safe-conduct for his person from the magnanimous and most illustrious six-or-seven-times-honored captain-general of the Greek army, Agamemnon, et cetera. Do this."

"Jove bless great Ajax!" Patroclus said.

"Hmm!" Thersites replied in the character of Ajax.

"I come from the worthy Achilles —" Patroclus began.

"Ha!"

"— who most humbly desires you to invite Hector to his tent —"

"Hmm!"

"— and to procure safe-conduct from Agamemnon."

"Agamemnon!"

"Yes, my lord."

"Ha!"

"What do you say to this request?"

"God be with you, with all my heart, and goodbye," Thersites replied in the character of Ajax.

"What is your answer, sir?" Patroclus asked.

"If tomorrow is a fair day, by eleven o'clock it will go one way or the other, and we will know who has won the duel; howsoever it turns out, Hector shall receive a beating before he beats me."

"What is your answer, sir?" Patroclus asked again.

"Fare you well, with all my heart, and goodbye," Thersites replied in the character of Ajax.

Achilles asked, "Why, but Ajax is not in this tune, is he? He isn't really in this state of mind, is he?"

"No, he is not in this tune, but he's out of tune just the way I have portrayed him," Thersites replied. "What music will be in him when Hector has knocked out his brains, I don't know; but, I am sure, none, unless the fiddler-god Apollo get Ajax' sinews to make musical strings from."

"Come, you shall carry a letter to Ajax immediately," Achilles said.

"Let me carry another letter to Ajax' horse; for that's the more capable creature," Thersites said.

"My mind is troubled, like a stirred fountain that is clouded with sediment," Achilles said, "and I myself cannot see its bottom."

Achilles and Patroclus exited.

Alone, Thersites said to himself, "I wish the fountain of your mind were clear again, so that I might bring to drink an ass — Ajax — at it! I had rather be a tick on a sheep than such a valiant ignorant fool as Ajax."

CHAPTER 4
— 4.1 —

On a street in Troy, Aeneas and a servant with a torch met Paris, Deiphobus, Antenor, the Greek Diomedes, and some other people who were carrying torches.

Paris said, "I see someone. Ho! Who is that there?"

"It is the Lord Aeneas," Deiphobus said.

Aeneas asked, "Is Prince Paris there in person? Had I as good a reason as Helen to lie long in bed as you, Prince Paris, have, nothing but Heavenly business would rob my bedmate of my company."

"That's what I think, too," Diomedes said. "Good morning, Lord Aeneas."

"This is a valiant Greek, Aeneas," Paris said. "Shake his hand. Witness the theme of your speech, wherein you told how Diomedes, for a whole week of days, haunted you on the battlefield."

"I wish you good health, valiant sir, while talks continue during all this gentle truce," Aeneas said to Diomedes, "but when I meet you armed on the battlefield after the truce, then I will greet you with as black defiance as heart can think or courage can execute."

"I welcome both the good health and the black defiance," Diomedes replied. "Our emotions are now calm because of the truce, and for as long as the truce lasts, I wish you good health! But when we meet on the battlefield later, by Jove, I'll hunt for your life with all my strength, speed, and cunning."

"And you shall hunt a lion that will flee with his face backward, facing you," Aeneas said. "In humane gentleness, welcome to Troy! Now, by my mortal father Anchises' life, welcome, indeed! By my immortal mother Venus' hand, I swear that no man alive can respect more excellently than I the thing he means to kill."

As recounted in Homer's *Iliad*, Diomedes had once fought Venus, who was on the side of the Trojans, and wounded her wrist.

"We feel the same way," Diomedes said. "Jove, let Aeneas live, if he is not fated to bring me glory by dying on my sword, a thousand complete courses of the Sun! Let him live a thousand years if I do not kill him on the battlefield!

But, to increase my honor, which I am greedy for, let me kill him, with each of his joints wounded, and let that happen tomorrow!"

"We know each other well," Aeneas said.

"We do, and we long to know each other worse," Diomedes replied.

Rather than know each other to be well and healthy, they each hoped to know that the other was wounded or dead.

"This is the most despiteful gentle greeting, the noblest hateful love, that ever I heard of," Paris said.

He then asked Aeneas, "What business, lord, do you have so early?"

"King Priam sent for me," Aeneas said, "but why, I don't know."

"The reason meets you here and now," Paris said. "It was to bring this Greek, Diomedes, to Calchas' house, where Cressida, his daughter, is living, and there to render him, in exchange for the freed Antenor, the fair Cressida."

Paris then walked to the side with Aeneas, and they held a private, quiet conversation.

Paris said, "Let's have your company, or if you please, you can hasten to Calchas' house before us. I firmly think — or rather, call my thought a certain knowledge — that my brother Troilus lodges there tonight. Rouse him and give him notice of our approach. Because of the reason we are coming there, I fear we shall be much unwelcome."

"I assure you that we will be much unwelcome," Aeneas replied. "Troilus had rather Troy were carried to Greece than Cressida carried away from Troy."

"There is no help for it," Paris said. "The bitter disposition of the time will have it so. It is necessary."

Paris then said loudly, "Go on ahead of us, Aeneas; we'll follow you."

"Good morning, everyone," Aeneas said.

Aeneas and the servant carrying the torch exited.

Paris then asked, "Tell me, noble Diomedes, indeed, tell me truly, even in the soul of sound and good friendship, who, in your thoughts, deserves fair Helen best, myself or Menelaus?"

"Both of you deserve her equally," Diomedes said. "Menelaus well deserves to have her because he seeks her without being bothered by her dirty lack of chastity, which has caused such a Hell of pain and world of expense as we fight this war to get her back for him. And you deserve as well to keep her because you defend her without noticing the taste of her dishonor, her lack of faithfulness, her adultery, which has led to such a costly loss of wealth and friends.

"Menelaus, like a whining cuckold, would drink up the lees and dregs of a flat tamed piece — a wine that has been exposed to the air and gone flat, or a piece of female flesh that has been in bed with men so much that she has become stale.

"You, like a lecher, are happy to breed your inheritors — your children — out of Helen's whorish genitals.

"Weighing both merits with a set of scales, each weighs neither less nor more than the other, but both are heavier — sadder — because of a whore named Helen."

"You are too bitter to your countrywoman," Paris replied.

"Helen is bitter to her country," Diomedes said. "Listen to me, Paris. For every false drop in her bawdy veins a Greek's life has sunk and been lost; for every tiny bit of her contaminated carrion weight, a Trojan has been slain. Since Helen has been able to speak, the number of words she has spoken does not equal the number of Greeks and Trojans who have died in this war over her."

"Fair Diomedes, you are doing what merchants do," Paris said. "You dispraise the thing that you desire to buy. But we in silence hold this virtue well, we'll commend only what we intend to sell."

Paris did not commend — praise — Helen because he had no desire to sell her.

Paris said, "Here lies our way."

They then walked to Calchas' house.

Troilus and Cressida stood and talked in the courtyard of Calchas' house.

Troilus said, "Dear, do not trouble yourself. The morning is cold."

Now that it was morning, it was time for Troilus to leave. Cressida wanted to protect her reputation; she did not want other people to know that Troilus had spent the night with her.

"Then, my sweet lord, I'll call my uncle down," Cressida said. "He shall unbolt the gates to let you out."

Pandarus lived next to Cressida. The houses shared the same court and were adjoined.

"Don't trouble him," Troilus said. "Go to bed, to bed. Let sleep kill — overcome — those pretty eyes, and give as soft arrest to your senses as infants' senses that are empty of all thought!"

"Good morning, then," Cressida said.

"Please, go to bed now."

"Are you weary of me?"

"Oh, Cressida! Except that the busy day, awakened by the morning lark, has aroused the ribald crows, and dreaming night will hide our joys no longer, I would not go away from you."

"Night has been too brief," Cressida said.

"Damn the witch called night! With malignant people thinking evil thoughts at night, she stays as tediously as Hell and allows time to pass only slowly, but she flies past the grasps of love with wings more momentary-swift than thought. You will catch cold, and curse me."

"Please, tarry. Stay a while longer," Cressida said. "You men will never tarry. Oh, foolish Cressida! I might have still held off and not slept with you, and then you would have tarried. Listen! There's someone up."

Pandarus said from inside, "Why are all the doors open here?"

"It is your uncle," Troilus said.

"A pestilence on him!" Cressida said. "Now he will be mocking me. What a life I shall have!"

Pandarus entered the courtyard and said, "How are you now! How are you now! How go maidenheads? What is the price of virginity?"

Pretending not to recognize Cressida, who was no longer a virgin, he said to her, "Hey, you maiden! Where's Cressida, my niece?"

"Go hang yourself, you naughty mocking uncle!" Cressida said. "You bring me to do, and then you flout me, too."

One meaning of "to do" is "to have sex."

"To do what?" Pandarus said. "To do what? Let her say what! What have I brought you to do?"

"Come, come, curse your heart!" Cressida said. "You'll never be good, nor will you allow others to be good."

"Ha! Ha!" Pandarus laughed. "Alas, poor wretch! Ah, poor *chipochia*! Haven't you slept tonight?"

Chipochia was poorly pronounced Italian for "pussy."

Using baby talk, he said to her, "Would he, a naughty man, not let it sleep? May a bugbear take him!"

Cressida said to Troilus, "Didn't I tell you that he would tease me! I wish that he were knocked in the head!"

Knocking sounded on the door of the courtyard.

She said to Pandarus, "Who's that at the door? Good uncle, go and see."

She then said to Troilus, "My lord, come again into my bedchamber."

Cressida wanted him to go back to her bedchamber because she did not want him to be found with her. She wanted to keep their sexual relationship secret.

He smiled, and she said, "You smile and mock me, as if I meant naughtily, as if I wanted to have sex again with you."

Troilus laughed.

"Come, you are deceived. I am thinking of no such thing."

Knocking sounded again at the door.

"How earnestly they knock!" Cressida said. "Please, come inside. I would not for half of Troy have you seen here."

Troilus and Cressida exited.

"Who's there?" Pandarus said. "What's the matter? Will you beat down the door? What is it now! What's the matter?"

He opened the door, and Aeneas entered the courtyard.

"Good morning, my lord, good morning," Aeneas said.

"Who's there?" Pandarus asked. "My Lord Aeneas! I swear that I didn't know who you are. What news gets you up so early?"

"Isn't Prince Troilus here?" Aeneas asked.

"Here! What should he be doing here?" Pandarus asked, pretending to be surprised by the question.

"Come, he is here, my lord," Aeneas said. "Do not deny it. He needs to speak with me about a matter that is important to him."

"Troilus is here, you say?" Pandarus said. "It is more than I know, I'll be sworn. As for my own part, I came in late. What would he be doing here?"

"What? Do you mean *who* would he be doing here?" Aeneas asked. "Well, then. Come, come, you'll do him wrong without meaning to. You'll be so true to him that you will be false to him. By trying to help him by pretending that he is not here, you will hurt him by keeping me from talking with him. Let's agree to pretend that you do not know about him being here, but still go and fetch him here; go."

Troilus, who had been eavesdropping, came out into the courtyard.

"How are you now?" Troilus asked Aeneas. "What's the matter?"

"My lord, I scarcely have leisure to greet you because my business with you is so urgent. Nearby are your brother Paris, and Deiphobus, the Greek Diomedes, and our Antenor, who has been freed by the Greeks and delivered to us; and for him forthwith, before the first sacrifice, within this hour, we must hand over to Diomedes' hand the Lady Cressida. She is being exchanged for Antenor."

"Has this been definitely decided?" Troilus asked.

"Yes, it has been decided by Priam and the general assembly of Troy. People are at hand and ready to put the decision into effect."

"How my achievements mock me!" Troilus said.

He had just won Cressida, and now he had to give her up.

He continued, "I will go and meet them, and, my Lord Aeneas, say that we met by chance; you did not find me here."

"Yes, that is a good idea, my lord," Aeneas said. "The secrets of nature are not more gifted in taciturnity than I am. Nature holds on to her secrets, and I will hold on to your secret."

Troilus and Aeneas exited.

Pandarus said, "Is it possible? No sooner gotten but lost? May the Devil take Antenor! The young Prince Troilus will go mad: a plague upon Antenor! I wish the Greeks had broken his neck!"

Cressida came into the courtyard and asked, "What's going on! What's the matter? Who was here?"

Pandarus sighed.

"Why do you sigh so deeply?" Cressida asked. "Where's my lord? Gone! Tell me, sweet uncle, what's the matter?"

"I wish that I were as deep under the earth as I am above it!"

"Oh, the gods! What's the matter?"

"Please, go inside," Pandarus said. "I wish that you had never been born! I knew you would be Troilus' death. Oh, poor gentleman! A plague upon Antenor!"

"Good uncle, I beg you, on my knees!" Cressida said. "I beg you, tell me what's the matter."

"You must leave Troy, girl, you must leave Troy; you have been exchanged for Antenor," Pandarus said. "You must go to your father, and be gone from Troilus. It will be his death; it will be his bane, his poison, his ruin; he cannot bear it."

"Oh, you immortal gods!" Cressida said. "I will not go."

"You must."

"I will not, uncle," Cressida said. "I have forgotten my father; I know no feeling of blood relationship to him; I know no sense of relationship, love, blood, soul for him that comes close to what I feel for the sweet Troilus. Oh, you divine gods, make Cressida's name the very crown of falsehood if she ever leaves Troilus! Time, force, and death, do to this body what extremes you can, but the strong base and building of my love is like the very center of the Earth, and draws all things to it. I'll go in and weep —"

"Do, do," Pandarus said.

Cressida continued, "— tear my bright hair and scratch my praised cheeks, crack my clear voice with sobs and break my heart with calling the name of Troilus. I will not go away from Troy."

Paris, Troilus, Aeneas, Deiphobus, Antenor, and the Greek Diomedes walked to the street in front of Calchas' house. Paris and Troilus stood apart from the others.

Paris said loudly, "It is full morning, and the hour fixed for Cressida's delivery to this valiant Greek, Diomedes, is coming quickly."

He and Troilus then talked quietly.

"My good brother Troilus, tell the lady what she is to do, and urge her to make haste."

"Walk into her house," Troilus said. "I'll bring her to the Greek quickly, and when I deliver her to his hand, think that his hand is an altar and your brother Troilus is a priest there who is offering to it his own heart."

Paris said, "I know what it is to love, and I wish that I could help as much as I shall feel pity!"

Troilus exited.

Paris said loudly, "May it please you to walk into her house, my lords."

Pandarus and Cressida were talking inside her house.

"Be calm, be calm," Pandarus advised.

"Why are you telling me to be calm?" Cressida said. "The grief that I taste is pure and entirely perfect, and it rages as strongly as that which causes it, so how can I moderate it? How can I be calm? If I could moderate my affection, or brew it for a weak and colder palate, then I could give my grief some moderation that would weaken the senses. My love for Troilus, however, admits no qualifying impure dross; and neither does my grief because it suffers such a precious loss."

"Here, here, here he comes," Pandarus said.

Troilus entered the room, and Pandarus said affectionately, "Ah, sweet ducks!"

"Oh, Troilus! Troilus!" Cressida said as she embraced him.

"What a pair of sights is here!" Pandarus said. "Let me hug, too."

He put his arms around both of them and hugged them and then said, "'Oh, heart,' as the goodly saying is, '— oh, heart, heavy and sorrowful heart, why do you sigh without breaking?' Where he answers again, 'Because you cannot ease your smart — your hurt — by friendship or by speaking.'"

Pandarus paused and then said, "There was never a truer rhyme. Let us cast away nothing, for we may live to have need of such a verse. We see it happen. We see the need for it. How are you doing now, lambs?"

"Cressida, I love you in so distilled and pure a way that the blessed gods are angry with my love for you, which is brighter in zeal than the devotion that cold lips blow in prayers to their deities," Troilus said. "That is why the gods are taking you from me."

"Have the gods envy and jealousy?" Cressida asked.

"Yes, yes, yes, yes," Pandarus said. "It is all too plainly the case here."

Cressida asked, "And is it true that I must go away from Troy?"

"It is a hateful truth," Troilus said.

"And from Troilus, too?" Cressida asked.

Troilus replied, "Yes, from Troy and Troilus."

"Is it possible?" she asked.

"Yes, and it has happened suddenly," Troilus said. "The injury of chance events — bad luck — refuses to give us time to properly say goodbye. The injury of chance events jostles roughly by all time of pause and rudely beguiles our lips of all reunions and kisses, it forcibly prevents our arms from locking in embraces, and it strangles our dear vows even in the birth of our own laboring breath — it cuts off the vows we attempt to make to each other even before we can say them. We two, who bought each other with so many thousand sighs, must sell ourselves at a cheap price with the rude brevity and discharge of only one sigh. Injurious time now with a robber's haste stuffs his rich thievery willy-nilly in a small sack. As many farewells as there are stars in Heaven, each farewell with its own distinct breath and kisses, he fumbles up into a casual *adieu*, and scants us with a single famished kiss, which tastes of the salt of the tears of broken lovers."

Aeneas called from outside the room, "My lord, is the lady ready?"

"Listen," Troilus said. "He is calling for you. Some say the Genius similarly cries, 'Come,' to the man who immediately must die."

The Genius is a Guardian Spirit that accompanies a human being during life and then guides the soul to its abode after death.

Troilus called to Aeneas, "Tell them to be patient; she shall come quickly."

Pandarus said, "Where are my tears? Rain, tears, to slow down this wind — my sighs — or my heart will be blown up by the root."

Pandarus was referring to the belief that rain causes a wind to slow down.

Pandarus exited.

Cressida asked Troilus, "Must I then go to the Greeks?"

"There's no remedy. There's no alternative," Troilus replied.

"I will be a woeful Cressida among the merry Greeks!" she said.

One meaning of "merry Greeks" in this culture was "dissolute and wanton rogues."

She continued, "When shall we see each other again?"

Troilus said, "Listen to me, my love. Be true —"

"To be true" means "to be faithful and not fall in love with someone else."

"Can you doubt that I will be true! What! What wicked thought is this?"

"We must use remonstrations kindly because we are parting and will be unable to speak to each other. I say, 'Be true,' not because I fear that you intend to be otherwise, for I will throw my glove to and challenge Death himself so I can prove by force of arms that there's no stain in your heart. But I say, 'Be true,' to introduce my following words: 'Be true, and I will see you.'"

"Oh, if you go to the Greek camp, you shall be exposed, my lord, to dangers as infinite as they are imminent!" Cressida said. "But I'll be true."

"And I'll become friends with danger," Troilus said. "Wear this sleeve."

In this culture, sleeves were detachable from the rest of the upper garment. They were sometimes given as love tokens.

"And you wear this glove," Cressida said, giving him a glove as he gave her the sleeve. "When shall I see you?"

Both garments — sleeve and glove — had holes into which one or more phallic-like objects could be thrust.

"I will corrupt — bribe — the Greek sentinels so I can visit you at night. But yet be true."

"Oh, Heavens! 'Be true' again!"

"Pay attention as I explain why I speak those words, love," Troilus said. "The Greek youths are full of good qualities. They're loving, well composed with gifts of nature such as good looks, and flowing and swelling over with arts and exercise: They have studied and practiced arts that make them attractive. How novelty and good qualities with a fine figure may move a woman — alas, a kind of godly jealousy, which I beg you to call a virtuous sin, makes me afraid."

Understanding that Troilus was afraid that she would fall in love with a Greek, Cressida said, "Oh, Heavens! You don't love me!"

"May I die a villain, then!" Troilus said. "In saying these things, I do not call your faith in question as much as I call into question my merit: I cannot sing, nor dance the high-jumping dance called the lavolt, nor sweeten my talk, nor play at crafty games; these are all fair virtues that the Greeks are most prompt and ready to practice. But I can tell that in each of these virtues there lurks a still and dumb-discursive — that is, a still and silently persuasive — Devil that tempts most cunningly, but don't you be tempted."

"Do you think I will be tempted?" Cressida asked.

"No, but something may be done that we will not."

Troilus was using "will" to mean "wish."

He continued, "And sometimes we are Devils to ourselves, when we tempt the frailty of our powers, presuming on their changeful potency. Sometimes, we rely too much on our own strength, but our strength can grow weak."

Aeneas called again, "It's time, my good lord."

"Come, kiss me," Troilus said, "and let us part."

Paris called, "Brother Troilus!"

Troilus called back, "Good brother, come here, and bring Aeneas and the Greek with you."

"My lord, will you be true to me?" Cressida asked.

"Who, I? Unfortunately, being true is my vice, my fault. While others fish with cunning to get a great reputation for a good character, I with great truth catch total simplicity. Because I tell the truth, I get a reputation for being simple — a fool. While some with cunning gild their copper crowns to make them appear to be gold, with truth and plainness I wear my crown bare."

The crowns were both coins and the tops of heads. Unlike some other people, Troilus did not put on an act to make himself look gilded — better than he really was.

He added, "Fear not my truth — my faithfulness to you. The moral of my intelligence is 'plain and true'; that's all there is to my character."

Aeneas, Paris, Antenor, Deiphobus, and the Greek Diomedes entered the room.

Troilus said, "Welcome, Sir Diomedes! Here is the lady whom we deliver to you in exchange for Antenor. At the city gate, lord, I'll give her into your hand, and as we walk to the gate I'll tell you about her. Treat her well; and, by my soul, fair Greek, if ever you stand at the mercy of my sword, say the name 'Cressida' and your life shall be as safe as Priam is in Troy."

Diomedes said, "Fair Lady Cressida, if it pleases you, save the thanks this Prince expects. You owe him nothing. The luster in your eyes and the Heaven in your cheeks plead for you to be treated well, and you shall be my mistress and command Diomedes wholly."

Diomedes was using courtly language. "Mistress" meant a woman who could command a man — called her "servant" — to do things for her because the man admired her; however, another meaning of "mistress" in this culture was "a woman who is pursued by a man."

"Greek, you are not treating me with courtesy," Troilus said. "Instead, by praising her you shame the zeal of my petition to you. I tell you, lord of Greece, she is as far high soaring over your praises as you are unworthy to be called her servant. I order you to treat her well simply for the reason that I have ordered you to treat her well. For, by the dreadful Pluto, god of the Land of the Dead, if you do not treat her well, even if the great bulk of Achilles is your bodyguard, I'll cut your throat."

"Oh, don't be angry, Prince Troilus," Diomedes replied. "Let me be privileged by my position as ambassador and messenger to speak freely: When I am away from Troy, I'll answer to my lust."

"I'll answer to my lust" can mean several things: 1) "I'll do as I like," 2) "I'll meet you on the battlefield," 3) "I'll treat Cressida well simply because I want to, not because you order me to," and/or 4) "I'll seduce Cressida."

Diomedes continued, "You should know, lord, that I'll do nothing because I have been ordered to do it. Cressida shall be prized according to her own worth. If you tell me, 'Prize her because I tell you to prize her,' I'll reply in accordance with my spirit and honor, 'No.'"

"Come, let's go to the gate," Troilus said. "I'll tell you, Diomedes, this boast of yours shall often make you hide your head."

He then said to Cressida, "Lady, give me your hand, and, as we walk, we shall say to each other what needs to be said."

Troilus, Cressida, and Diomedes exited.

A trumpet sounded.

Paris said, "Listen! That is Hector's trumpet."

"How we have spent this morning! We have wasted time," Aeneas said. "Prince Hector must think that I am tardy and remiss. I swore that I would ride before him to the battlefield."

"It is Troilus' fault that handing over Cressida to Diomedes took so long," Paris said. "Come, let's go to the battlefield with Hector."

"Let's get ready immediately," Aeneas said.

"Yes, let's get ready with a bridegroom's fresh eagerness," Paris said. "Let us prepare to tend on Hector's heels. The glory of our Troy lies this day on his fair worth and single chivalry. This is the day that he will fight a duel with Ajax."

Ajax, wearing armor, walked over to Agamemnon, Achilles, Patroclus, Menelaus, Ulysses, Nestor, and some others. They were at the place where Ajax would duel Hector. The lists — barriers surrounding the place where the duel would take place — were already set out.

Agamemnon said to Ajax, "Here you are wearing fresh and fair armor, early for the duel, and with abundant courage. Give with your trumpeter a loud note to Troy, you awe-inspiring Ajax, so that the appalled air may pierce the ears of the great combatant Hector and bring him hither."

"Trumpeter, here's some money," Ajax said. "Now crack your lungs, and split your brazen pipe. Blow, villain, until your sphered and swollen cheeks outswell the gassy colic of the puffing Aquilon — the North Wind. Come, stretch your chest and let your eyes spout blood with the effort of blowing. You blow to summon Hector."

A trumpet sounded.

"No trumpet answers," Ulysses said.

"It is still early," Achilles said.

Seeing two people coming toward them, Agamemnon asked, "Isn't that Diomedes yonder, with Calchas' daughter?"

"It is Diomedes," Ulysses said. "I know the manner of his gait. He rises on the toe: His aspiring spirit lifts him from the earth."

Diomedes led Cressida over to Agamemnon.

"Is this the Lady Cressida?" Agamemnon asked.

"Yes, it is she," Diomedes replied.

"You are very dearly welcome to the Greeks, sweet lady," Agamemnon said, kissing her.

"Our general salutes you with a kiss," Nestor said.

"Yet the kindness is only particular," Ulysses said. "It would be better if she were kissed in general."

"That is very courtly counsel," Nestor, who was an old man, said. "I'll begin."

He kissed Cressida and said, "So much for Nestor."

Referring to Nestor's old age — he was in the December of his life — Achilles said, "I'll take that winter from your lips, fair lady."

He kissed her and said, "Achilles bids you welcome."

"I had a good argument for kissing once," Menelaus said.

By "argument," he meant "cause or reason." That argument was Helen.

"But that's no argument for kissing now," Patroclus said, using "argument" with its usual meaning.

He kissed Cressida and said, "For thus popped Paris in his hardiment, and parted thus you and your argument."

Patroclus was making fun of Menelaus, whose wife, Helen, was sleeping with Paris, Prince of Troy. "Hardiment" is an archaic word meaning "act of valor" and "erect penis." "Pop in" means to "arrive unexpectedly" and "move in suddenly." Paris had popped in to visit Menelaus, King of Sparta, and he had popped his erect penis into Helen.

"Oh, this is deadly gall, and the theme of all our scorns!" Ulysses said. "For this we lose our heads to gild his horns."

Menelaus was a cuckold, a man with an unfaithful wife. Cuckolds were said to have horns. By fighting the Trojan War to get Helen back for Menelaus, the Greeks were fighting to gild his horns — to get back some of the honor that Paris had taken from him.

"The first kiss I gave you was Menelaus' kiss," Patroclus said. "This kiss is mine."

He kissed Cressida and said, "Patroclus kisses you."

"Oh, this is excellent!" Menelaus said, sarcastically.

Patroclus said, "Paris and I kiss evermore for Menelaus."

Paris kissed Helen for Menelaus, and now Patroclus was kissing Cressida for Menelaus.

"I'll have my kiss, sir," Menelaus said to Patroclus.

He then said to Cressida, "Lady, by your leave."

Cressida was a young Trojan woman who was surrounded by Greek men in what could very well be a dangerous situation for her.

Silent up to now, Cressida said to Menelaus, "In kissing, do you give or receive?"

Menelaus said, "I both take and give."

Cressida said, "I'll bet my life that the kiss you take is better than the kiss you give; therefore, you get no kiss.'

"I'll give you something in addition," Menelaus said. "I'll give you three kisses in return for one kiss."

"You're an odd man," Cressida said. "Give even odds or give none."

By "odd," Cressida meant "eccentric or unusual."

"An odd man, lady!" Menelaus said. "Every man is odd."

Menelaus was saying that every man is a unique individual.

"No, Paris is not," Cressida said, "for you know it is true that you are odd, and he is even with you."

Cressida was saying that Paris was even because he was part of a couple, while Menelaus was odd — a single man who was odd man out and who was at odds with Paris.

Menelaus replied, "You hit me on the head."

Cressida's comments were cutting him close to the bone — she was hitting him on his cuckold's horns.

"No, I'll be sworn," Cressida said.

"It is no contest, your fingernail against his horn," Ulysses said. "His horns are tougher than your fingernails."

He then asked, "May I, sweet lady, beg a kiss of you?"

"You may," Cressida replied.

"I do desire a kiss."

"Why, beg, then."

Ulysses, who was unwilling to beg in any serious way, said, "Why then for Venus' sake, give me a kiss when Helen is a maiden — a virgin — again, and when she belongs to Menelaus again."

Helen would never be a virgin again, and having cuckolded Menelaus, would she ever really be his again?

"I am your debtor," Cressida said. "Claim your kiss when it is due."

"Never is my day to claim my kiss, and then I will get a kiss of you," Ulysses said.

Cressida had managed to use her wits to avoid being kissed by Menelaus and by Ulysses.

Diomedes said to her, "Lady, a word. I'll bring you to your father."

Diomedes and Cressida exited.

Nestor said, "She is a woman of quick sense."

"Sense" could mean "wits" or "sensuality."

"Damn her!" Ulysses, who had not received a kiss, said. "There's language in her eye, her cheek, her lip — you can read her or listen to her. Her foot speaks; her wanton spirits appear in every joint and motion of her body. Oh, these flirts, so glib of tongue, who accost men and give them welcome before they come near, and widely unclasp the tablets of their thoughts to every ticklish, lecherous reader! Set them down for sluttish spoils of opportunity and daughters of the game. Set them down in the records as the whores they are."

Was Ulysses accurate in thinking that Cressida was a slut? Or was he just angry at not having received a kiss?

A trumpet sounded.

All the Greeks said, "The Trojans' trumpet."

Or perhaps they said, in response to Ulysses' words, "The Trojan strumpet."

"Yonder comes the Trojans' troop," Agamemnon said.

Hector, along with Aeneas, Troilus, and other Trojan soldiers and some attendants, walked over to the Greeks. Hector was wearing armor.

"Hail, all you rulers of Greece!" Aeneas said. "What shall be done to him who commands victory? What shall the victor win? Or do you purpose that a victor shall be known? Do you want the knights to fight to the death, or shall the knights be separated before death occurs by any voice or order of the marshal of the lists? Hector bade me ask you this."

"Which way would Hector have it?" Agamemnon asked.

"He has no preference," Aeneas replied. "He'll obey whatever conditions you set."

Achilles said, "This is done like Hector; but it is done overconfidently. It is done a little proudly, and a great deal disparaging the knight opposing Hector."

Aeneas asked, "If not Achilles, sir, what is your name?"

"If not Achilles, my name is nothing," Achilles replied.

"Therefore your name is Achilles," Aeneas said, "but, whatever it is, know this: In the extremity of great and little, valor and pride excel themselves in Hector. The one is almost as infinite as all; the other is blank as nothing. He has much courage and is not at all proud. Weigh him well, and you will see that what looks like pride is courtesy. This Ajax is half made of Hector's blood. Out of love for that half, half of Hector stays at home; half heart, half hand, half Hector comes to seek this blended knight who is half Trojan and half Greek."

Hector and Ajax were first cousins. Ajax' mother was Hesione, who was the sister of Priam, Hector's father.

Achilles said sarcastically, "A maiden battle, then? Not a fight to the death? No bloodshed? Oh, I see."

Having delivered Cressida to Calchas, her father, Diomedes returned.

"Here is Sir Diomedes," Agamemnon said. "Go, honorable knight, and stand by our Ajax. As you and Lord Aeneas consent upon the order of their fight, so be it. The fight can be either to the uttermost — to the death — or else it can be exercise. Because the combatants are related by blood, their fight is half restrained before their strokes begin."

Ajax and Hector entered the lists; they were ready to duel.

"They are opposed already," Ulysses said.

Seeing Troilus, Agamemnon asked Ulysses, "What Trojan is that one who looks so sorrowful?"

"He is the youngest son of Priam, and he is a true knight. He is not yet fully mature, yet he is matchless and firm of word. He does his speaking with his deeds, and he does not boast about his deeds with his tongue. He is not soon provoked, but once he is provoked he is not soon calmed. His heart and hand are both open and both free and both generous; for what he has he gives, and what he thinks he shows. Yet he does not give until his rational judgment guides his bounty, nor does he dignify an impure thought by saying it out loud. He is as manly as Hector, but more dangerous; for Hector in his blaze of wrath shows mercy to tender objects that arouse his pity, but this man, the youngest son of Priam, in the heat of action is more vindictive than jealous love. They call him Troilus, and on him erect a second hope, as fairly built as Hector. They think of him as an up-and-coming second Hector. Thus says Aeneas, who knows the youth from top to bottom; from his heart Aeneas thus described Troilus to me when I was an ambassador inside Troy."

Trumpets sounded, and Hector and Ajax began to duel. The marshals of the duel were Aeneas and Diomedes.

"They are in action," Agamemnon said.

"Now, Ajax, hold your own!" Nestor shouted.

"Hector, you are asleep!" Troilus shouted. "Wake up!"

"His blows are well placed," Agamemnon said to Nestor.

Agamemnon shouted, "There, Ajax!"

Diomedes said to Hector and Ajax, "You must fight no more."

The trumpeters stopped blowing.

"Princes, enough, if it pleases you," Aeneas said.

"I am not warm yet," Ajax said. "I haven't broken a sweat. Let us fight again."

"Whatever Hector pleases," Diomedes replied.

"Why, then I fight no more today," Hector said to Diomedes.

He then said to Ajax, "You are, great lord, my father's sister's son, a first cousin to me, the son of great Priam. The obligation of our blood relation forbids a gory rivalry between us two. Were your Greek and Trojan mixture such that you could say, 'This hand is all Greek, and this hand is all Trojan; the muscles of this leg are all Greek, and the muscles of this leg are all Trojan; my mother's blood runs here on the right cheek, and my father's blood runs here on the left cheek,' then by most powerful Jove, you would not go away from me bearing a Greek limb or other body part in which my sword had not made its mark during our violent duel, but the just gods forbid that any drop of blood you got from your mother, my sacred aunt, should by my mortal sword be drained from your body! Let me embrace you, Ajax. By Jove who thunders, you have strong arms."

Hector hugged Ajax and said, "Hector would have your strong arms fall upon him like this. Cousin, I give all honor to you!"

"I thank you, Hector," Ajax said. "You are too gentle, too noble, and too free a man. I came to kill you, cousin, and bear away from here a great addition to my honor — a great addition earned by your death."

Hector replied, "Not even the admirable Pyrrhus Neoptolemus, Achilles' son — on whose bright crest Fame loudly cried, 'Oyez — hear me — this is he,' could promise to himself a thought of added honor torn from Hector. Not even the admirable Neoptolemus can promise to himself that he will be able to kill me and to take my honor for himself."

"Soldiers from both sides are expectantly awaiting what you will do," Aeneas said.

"We'll let them know," Hector said. "The conclusion of the duel is a hug."

He added, "Ajax, farewell."

Ajax replied, "If I might in my entreaties find success — as I seldom have the chance to ask you this — I would like you, my famous cousin, to visit our Greek tents."

"It is Agamemnon's wish," Diomedes said, "and great Achilles longs to see unarmed the valiant Hector."

"Aeneas, call my brother Troilus to me," Hector said, "and report this friendly face-to-face meeting between me and the Greeks to the Trojans who are awaiting news. Request that they return to Troy."

He then said to Ajax, "Shake hands with me, my cousin. I will go and eat with you and see your knights."

Agamemnon came forward.

Ajax said, "Great Agamemnon comes to meet us here."

Hector said to Ajax, "Tell me name by name the worthiest of them except for Achilles because my own searching eyes shall find him by his large and imposing size."

Hector did not recognize many of the Greeks because on the battlefield, the soldiers wore helmets. Ulysses and Diomedes, however, had been ambassadors to Troy, and so Hector recognized them, and they recognized many of the Trojans.

Agamemnon said to Hector, "You are worthy of arms!"

Agamemnon hugged Hector. Agamemnon's words had two meanings: 1) Hector was worthy of being hugged. 2) Hector was worthy of his armor and weapons.

Agamemnon added, "You are as welcome as you can be to one who would be rid of such an enemy — but that's no welcome. Understand more clearly: Both what's past and what's to come are strewn with husks and the formless ruin of oblivion, but in this existing moment, my good faith and trustworthiness, strained pure from all insincere crooked-dealing, bid you, with the most divine integrity, from the bottom of my heart, great Hector, welcome."

"I thank you, most imperial Agamemnon," Hector said.

Agamemnon said to Troilus, "My well-famed lord of Troy, I give no less welcome to you."

"Let me confirm my Princely brother's greeting," Menelaus said. "You pair of warlike brothers, welcome hither."

"Who must we answer?" Hector asked Aeneas. Hector did not recognize Menelaus.

Aeneas replied, "He is the noble Menelaus."

"Oh, you are Menelaus, my lord?" Hector said. "By Mars' gauntlet, I thank you! Don't mock me because I use the fancy oath 'by Mars' gauntlet,' which I seldom use. Your former wife swears still by Venus' glove that she's well, but she bade me not to commend her to you."

Hector was subtly mocking the cuckold Menelaus by bringing up Mars, god of war, and Venus, goddess of sexual passion, who had had an affair together, thereby cuckolding Venus' husband, Vulcan.

"Don't name her now, sir," Menelaus said, referring to Helen. "She's a deadly theme."

"Pardon me," Hector said. "I have offended you."

Nestor said, "I have, you gallant Trojan, seen you often, laboring for fate, make your cruel way through ranks of young Greek soldiers, and I have seen you, as hot as Perseus, who slew the Gorgon Medusa, who had snakes for hair, spur your Trojan steed, despising many soldiers whom you had defeated and who had thereby forfeited their lives, when you have hung your advanced sword in the air and not let it fall on the fallen. Then I have said to some people standing by me, 'Look, Jupiter is yonder, dealing life to those from whom he could take life!' And I have seen you pause and take your breath, when a ring of Greeks has hemmed you in, as if they were watching a wrestler in a match at the Olympics. These things I have seen. But this your countenance, which has always been locked in a steel helmet, I never saw till now.

"I knew your grandfather Laomedon, and I once fought with him. He was a good soldier, but by great Mars, the captain of us all, I have never seen a soldier like you. Let an old man embrace you, and, worthy warrior, I bid you welcome to our tents."

Actually Nestor had fought *against* Hector's grandfather, but Nestor used the word *with*, which was accurate but less likely to cause offense due to ambiguity: To fight "with" could mean to fight "against" or to fight "on the side of." Nestor addressed Hector in a friendly manner, as did Hector when he replied to Nestor.

"He is the old Nestor," Aeneas said to Hector.

"Let me embrace you, good old chronicle," Hector said. "You are a living history book because you have lived so long — you have for so long walked hand in hand with time. Most revered Nestor, I am glad to hug you."

"I wish my arms could match you in contention — in a battle — as they contend now with you in courtesy and etiquette," Nestor said.

"I wish they could," Hector said.

"Ha! By this white beard, I would fight with you tomorrow," Nestor said. "Well, welcome, welcome! I have seen the time when I was young enough to fight you on the battlefield, but that time is past."

"I wonder now how yonder city stands when we have here her base and pillar by us," Ulysses said. "The very foundation of Troy is here in the Greek camp."

"I know your face, Lord Ulysses, well," Hector said. "Ah, sir, there's many a Greek and Trojan dead, since I first saw you and Diomedes in Troy, while you two were on your Greek embassy."

When the Greeks first arrived at Troy, they conquered Tenedos, an island lying near Troy, and then they sent Ulysses and Diomedes on an embassy to Troy, unsuccessfully hoping to get Helen and reparations.

"Sir, I foretold to you then what would ensue," Ulysses said. "My prophecy is but half fulfilled yet. In order for my prophecy to be fulfilled, yonder walls, which boldly stand in front of your town, and yonder towers, whose wanton tops kiss the clouds, must kiss their own feet. In order for my prophecy to be fulfilled, Troy's walls and towers must fall."

"I must not believe you," Hector said. "That will never happen. Troy's walls and towers stand there yet, and modestly, I think, the fall of every Trojan stone will cost a drop of Greek blood. The end of this war will tell all, and that old resolver of all quarrels, Time, will one day end this war."

"So to Time we leave it," Ulysses said. "Most noble and most valiant Hector, welcome. After you feast with the general, Agamemnon, I ask that you next feast with me and see me in my tent."

Achilles interrupted: "I shall forestall thee, Lord Ulysses, thou! Now, Hector, I have fed my eyes on thee. I have with exact view perused thee, Hector, and examined thee joint by joint."

Achilles was being rude. He was using the familiar "thee" to refer to Ulysses, an older man to whom he ought to show respect, and he was using the familiar "thee" to refer to Hector, an honored guest in the Greek camp. Achilles should have used the formal "you" to refer to both men.

"Is this Achilles?" Hector asked.

"I am Achilles."

"Stand in full view, I ask thee," Hector said. "Let me look on thee."

Hector was irritated by Achilles and so called him "thee." Previously, Hector and Ulysses had respectfully called each other "you."

Achilles came forward and said, "Behold thy fill."

"No, I am done already," Hector said.

"Thou are too brief," Achilles said. "I will look at thee a second time, as if I were going to buy thee. I will view thee limb by limb."

Achilles' words contained a suggestion of buying and then butchering an animal.

Angry and using the less respectful words "thou" and "thine," Hector said, "Oh, like a book on sport thou shall read me over. But there's more in me than you understand. Why do thou so stare at me with thine eye?"

Achilles got on his knees to pray to the gods and said, "Tell me, you Heavens, in which part of Hector's body shall I destroy him?"

He pointed to various parts of Hector's body and said, "Whether there, or there, or there? So that I may give the local wound a name and make distinct the very breach from out of which Hector's great spirit flew, answer me, Heavens!"

"It would discredit the blest gods, proud man, to answer such a question," Hector said. "Stand up again."

Achilles stood up.

Hector asked, "Do thou think that thou can catch my life so pleasantly and easily that thou can name in advance and precisely where thou will hit and kill me?"

"I tell thee, yes," Achilles said.

"Even if thou were an oracle telling me this, I would not believe thee. Henceforth, guard thee well, for I'll not kill thee there, nor there, nor there," Hector said, pointing to various parts of Achilles' body, "but, by the forge that forged Mars' helmet, I'll kill thee everywhere, yes, over and over."

Hector paused, and then he said, "You wisest Greeks, pardon me for making this brag. Achilles' insolence draws foolish words from my lips, but I'll work hard to make my deeds to match these words, or may I never —"

Ajax interrupted, "Thou should not allow yourself to be angry, cousin. And you, Achilles, stop making these threats until either chance or purposeful action brings you to face Hector on the battlefield. You may have enough every day of Hector if you have the stomach to face him. The general assembly of Greek leaders, I fear, can scarcely persuade you to be at odds with him on the battlefield."

Ajax was treating his first cousin Hector correctly by using the familiar and less formal "thou" to refer to him, and he was treating Achilles correctly by using the formal and respectful "you" to refer to him. But he was also correctly pointing out that Achilles was staying in camp and not fighting on the battlefield.

Mollified by Ajax' words, Hector used the formal and respectful "you" to refer to Achilles: "I ask you to let us see you on the battlefield. We have had petty, paltry battles since you refused to fight for the Greeks."

Still disrespectful, Achilles replied, "Do thou entreat me, Hector? Tomorrow I will meet thee, and I will be as cruel as death; tonight we shall all be friends."

"Reach out thy hand, and we will shake on that meeting," Hector said.

They shook hands.

"First, all you lords of Greece, go to my tent," Agamemnon said. "There we will feast to the fullest. Afterwards, as Hector's leisure and your bounties shall concur together, individually entertain and treat him."

He then ordered, "Beat loud the drums and let the trumpets blow, so that this great soldier may his welcome know."

Everyone exited except Troilus and Ulysses.

Troilus asked, "My Lord Ulysses, tell me, please, in what place of the Greek camp does Calchas sleep?"

"He sleeps in Menelaus' tent, most Princely Troilus," Ulysses replied. "Diomedes feasts with him there tonight; Diomedes looks upon neither the Heavens nor the Earth, but bends all his gazes and amorous views on the fair Cressida."

"I shall, lord, be bound to you so much, if, after we depart from Agamemnon's tent, you take me there to Menelaus' tent."

"You shall command me, sir," Ulysses said. "I shall do what you ask. Now kindly tell me the reputation this Cressida had in Troy. Did she have a lover there who bewails her absence?"

"Oh, sir, people who display their scars and boast about them ought to be mocked," Troilus said. "Will you walk on, my lord? Cressida was loved, and she loved; she is loved, and she does love. But still sweet love is food for fortune's tooth."

CHAPTER 5

— 5.1 —

Achilles and Patroclus talked together in front of Achilles' tent.

Achilles said about Hector, "I'll heat his blood with Greek wine tonight, and tomorrow with my curved sword I'll cool his blood by making it spurt from his body. Patroclus, let us feast him to the uttermost tonight."

"Here comes Thersites," Patroclus replied.

Thersites walked over to the two men.

"Hello, now, you core of envy!" Achilles said. "You crusty botch of nature, what's the news?"

Achilles was insulting Thersites by calling him a boil — a botch — that had crusted over. The core was the center of the boil.

"Why, you picture of what you seem to be, and idol of idiot worshippers, here's a letter for you," Thersites said.

Thersites had in return insulted Achilles by saying that Achilles had no substance. To Thersites, Achilles was all picture — all appearance — with nothing underneath.

"A letter from where, fragment?" Achilles asked.

A fragment was a small piece of food.

"Why, you full dish of fool, from Troy," Thersites replied.

"Who keeps the tent now?" Patroclus asked.

Previously, Achilles had kept to his tent and stayed close to it or in it, but now things seemed to be in motion for him to go to the battlefield in the morning and fight Hector. Now, Thersites kept — cleaned — the tent.

Deliberately misunderstanding the word "tent" to mean a surgeon's probe for wounds, Thersites replied, "The surgeon's box, or the patient's wound."

"Well said, Adversity!" Patroclus said. "And what is the need for you to use these tricks of wordplay?"

"Please, be silent, boy," Thersites said. "I do not profit by your talk. You are thought to be Achilles' male varlet."

More insults: "boy" and "male varlet."

"Male varlet, you rogue!" Patroclus said. "What's that?"

"Why, you are Achilles' masculine whore," Thersites said. "Now, may the rotten venereal diseases of the south, guts-griping hernias, colds and phlegm-producing illnesses, loads of kidney stones, unnatural drowsiness, cold paralysis of the limbs, sore eyes, dirt-rotten livers, wheezing lungs, bladders full of internal abscesses, sciaticas, psoriasis in the palm, incurable bone-ache, and wrinkle-causing chronic skin lesions take and take again — attack repeatedly — such absurd monstrosities as you!"

"Why, you damnable box of envy, thou, what do you mean by cursing like this?" Patroclus asked.

"Am I cursing you?" Thersites asked.

Patroclus was unwilling to admit that he was the target of these insults, so he replied, "Why, no, you ruinous butt, you bastard misshapen cur, no."

"No! Why are you then exasperated, you idle flimsy skein of silk thread, you green thin-silk flap for a sore eye, you tassel of a prodigal's purse, thou? Ah, how the poor world is pestered with such waterflies — mosquitoes, diminutives of nature!"

Thersites was gifted at invective. These insults compared Patroclus to flimsy decorations. A tassel is a hanging decoration, and a purse is a bag in which such things as precious stones can be carried. Thersites was calling Patroclus a penis and scrotum. But since the penis and scrotum belonged to a pauper, the penis was spent — limp — and the purse was empty.

"Get out, gall!" Patroclus shouted at Thersites.

"Finch-egg!" Thersites shouted at Patroclus.

Patroclus was much smaller than Achilles, and so many of Thersites' insults referred to Patroclus' diminutive stature. A finch and its egg are both small.

Achilles, who had been reading the letter he had received from Troy, interrupted the quarrel by saying, "My sweet Patroclus, I am thwarted entirely in my great plan to fight Hector in tomorrow's battle. Here is a letter from Queen Hecuba and a love token from Polyxena, her daughter, my fair love. Both Queen Hecuba and Polyxena are badgering me and requiring me to keep an oath that I have sworn. I will not break my oath. Let the Greeks fall in battle; let my reputation vanish, let my honor either go or stay — my major vow lies here, and this vow I'll obey."

Achilles had vowed not to fight the Trojans and to try to bring the Trojan War to a peaceful end because he had fallen in love with Polyxena.

Achilles then said, "Come, come, Thersites, help to straighten up my tent. This night in banqueting must all be spent. Let's go, Patroclus!"

Achilles and Patroclus exited.

Alone, Thersites said to himself, "With too much anger and too little brain, these two may run mad; but if they run mad with too much brain and too little anger, then I'll be a curer of madmen.

"Here's Agamemnon, an honest fellow enough and one who loves quails."

The word "quails" was used as slang for "prostitutes," as well as referring to the game birds.

Thersites continued, "But Agamemnon has not as much brain as he has earwax, and just consider the goodly transformation of Jupiter there, his brother, the bull — the primitive statue and oblique memorial of cuckolds."

Jupiter had transformed himself into a bull so that he could run away with the beautiful mortal woman Europa. Menelaus was similar to Jupiter's transformation because bulls have horns and Menelaus had the horns of a cuckold. However, Jupiter's transformation into a bull is only an "oblique memorial of cuckolds" because Jupiter was not a cuckold although he was wearing horns.

Thersites continued, "Menelaus is a thrifty shoeing-horn in a chain, hanging at his brother's leg."

Thersites was comparing Menelaus to a shoehorn, a curved tool used to help ease one's heel into a shoe. Menelaus' brother, Agamemnon, used Menelaus as a thrifty tool and so kept him nearby.

Consider this. Why would the Greeks and Trojans spend years fighting over Helen? Many warriors lost their lives, many Greek husbands were separated from their wives and children for years, and for many years, two groups of people were unable to do anything constructive such as build cities, raise herding animals, or grow crops. Thersites knew that Helen wasn't worth all this death, despair, and destruction, and therefore Agamemnon must be using Menelaus' cuckoldry as an excuse for attacking Troy in order to sack and take its treasures as the spoils of war.

In addition, Menelaus was like a tool hanging from Agamemnon's belt — he was a hanger-on.

Thersites continued, "Into what form should I transform Menelaus, other than what he is, if my wit could be intermingled with my malice and my malice stuffed with my wit? To transform Menelaus into an ass would be to do nothing; he is both ass and ox. He is a fool, and he is a horned cuckold. To transform him into an ox would be to do nothing; he is both ox and ass.

"How about if I were transformed? If I were to be a dog, a mule, a cat, a polecat, a toad, a lizard, an owl, a greedy puttock such as a hawk or kite, or a herring without a roe, I would not care; but if I were to be Menelaus, I would conspire against my destiny and resist it every way I could.

"Don't ask me what I would be if I were not Thersites, for I would not care if I were a louse on a leper, as long as I were not Menelaus!"

He saw some torches and said, "Hey-day! Spirits and fires!"

The torches were lighting the way of Hector, Troilus, Ajax, Agamemnon, Ulysses, Nestor, Menelaus, and Diomedes.

Some of the Greeks had had too much to drink, and they were lost in their own camp.

Agamemnon said, "We are going the wrong way. We are going the wrong way."

"No, yonder Achilles' tent is," Ajax said. "There, where we see the lights."

"I am a trouble to you," Hector said.

"No, not a whit," Ajax replied.

"Here comes Achilles himself to guide you," Ulysses said.

Achilles walked over to the group and said, "Welcome, brave Hector; welcome, all you Princes."

"So now, fair Prince of Troy," Agamemnon said to Hector, "I bid you good night. Ajax commands the guards who will see that you return safely to Troy."

"Thanks and good night to the Greeks' general," Hector said to Agamemnon.

"Good night, my lord," Menelaus said to Hector.

"Good night, sweet lord Menelaus," Hector replied.

"Sweet draught," Thersites said to himself. "'Sweet' says he! Sweet sink, sweet sewer."

The words "draught," "sink," and "sewer" all referred to cesspools and waste pits. Such was Thersites' opinion of Menelaus.

"Good night and welcome, both at once, to those who go or tarry," Achilles said.

"Good night," Agamemnon replied.

Agamemnon and Menelaus exited.

Achilles said, "Old Nestor tarries and stays here; and you also, Diomedes, should keep Hector company for an hour or two."

"I cannot, lord," Diomedes replied. "I have important business that I must attend to now."

He then said, "Good night, great Hector."

"Give me your hand," Hector said.

They shook hands.

Ulysses said quietly to Troilus, "Follow Diomedes' torch; he is going to Calchas' tent. I'll go with you and keep you company."

"Sweet sir, you honor me," Troilus said quietly to Ulysses.

"And so, good night," Hector said to Diomedes.

Diomedes exited. Ulysses and Troilus followed him.

Achilles said to his guests, "Come, come, enter my tent."

Achilles, Hector, Ajax, and Nestor entered Achilles' tent.

Alone, Thersites said to himself, "That same Diomedes is a false-hearted rogue, a most unjust scoundrel. I will no more trust him when he leers than I will trust a serpent when it hisses. Diomedes will open his mouth and make promises, exactly like Brabbler the hound that brays although it has no scent. But when Diomedes actually delivers on a promise, astronomers foretell it; it is a rare and unusual portent, and there will occur some major change in the world — the Sun borrows light from the Moon when Diomedes keeps his word."

Is Thersites always accurate in his assessment of other people? Doesn't Diomedes at least usually actually do what he says he will do?

Thersites continued, "I prefer to not see Hector than to not dog and follow Diomedes: They say that Diomedes keeps a Trojan whore, and uses the traitor Calchas' tent. I'll follow Diomedes. Nothing but lust and lechery! They are all unchaste varlets who cannot control their sexual urges!"

— 5.2 —

Diomedes walked over in front of Calchas' tent and called, "Are you still up? Speak to me."

From inside the tent, Calchas replied, "Who is calling?"

"I am Diomedes. You are Calchas, I think. Where's your daughter?"

From within the tent, Calchas said, "She will come out to you."

Troilus and Ulysses arrived, but they stayed out of sight of Diomedes. Thersites followed them, and he stayed out of sight of Diomedes as well as of Troilus and Ulysses.

Ulysses whispered to Troilus, "Stand where the torch will not reveal our presence."

Cressida came out of the tent.

Troilus said quietly, "Cressida comes forth to Diomedes."

"Hello, my charge!" Diomedes said to Cressida.

"Hello, my sweet guardian!" Cressida replied.

Diomedes had been given the task of taking Cressida out of Troy, and so for that period of time, at least, he had been her guardian and she had been his charge or responsibility.

Cressida said to Diomedes, "Listen, I want to have a word with you."

She whispered to him.

"They are so familiar with each other!" Troilus said.

"She will sing with any man at first sight," Ulysses replied.

He meant that Cressida would make advances to any man she saw. He also meant that she could look at a man and "read" him as if she were playing music at first sight, or sight-reading the music.

Thersites, who could hear what Troilus and Ulysses were saying, said to himself, "And any man may make music with her, if he can take her clef; she's noted."

The word "clef" referred to a musical note, but Thersites was punning on "cleft" — Cressida's vulva was cleft. By "noted," Thersites meant "notorious."

Diomedes said to Cressida, "Will you remember?"

"Remember?" Cressida replied. "Yes."

"Do it, and not just remember it," Diomedes said. "Let your mind be coupled with your words."

"What should she remember?" Troilus asked quietly.

"Listen," Ulysses replied.

"Sweet honey Greek, tempt me no more to sin," Cressida said.

"This is roguery!" Thersites said to himself.

"No, then —" Diomedes said.

"I'll tell you what —" Cressida began.

Diomedes interrupted, "Tell me nothing. You have forsworn yourself. You said that you would do it, but you won't do it."

"Truly, I cannot," Cressida said. "What then would you have me do?"

Thersites said to himself, "A juggling trick — to be secretly open."

Thersites understood Diomedes and Cressida to be talking about sex. The juggling trick would be for Cressida to pretend to be chaste in public while having an affair with Diomedes in private — Cressida would open her private parts for Diomedes secretly and in private.

Diomedes asked Cressida, "What did you swear you would bestow on me?"

"Please, do not hold me to my oath," Cressida said. "Bid me do anything but that, sweet Greek."

"Good night," Diomedes said curtly.

Troilus said, "Stop! Patience!"

Troilus was praying for calmness when he said, "Patience!"

"What is wrong, Trojan?" Ulysses asked Troilus.

"Diomedes —" Cressida began.

"No, no, good night," Diomedes replied. "I'll be your dupe no more."

Troilus said, "A better man than you will be her dupe."

Troilus was referring to himself.

"Listen," Cressida said. "Let me say one word in your ear."

"Oh, plague and madness!" Troilus said.

"You are angry, Prince," Ulysses said. "Let us depart, I beg you, lest your displeasure should grow and make you act in anger. This place is dangerous for you; the time is very deadly for you. I beg you, go now."

"Let's stay and watch, I beg you!" Troilus said.

"No, my good lord, leave now," Ulysses said. "Your anger is reaching high tide; come with me, my lord."

"Please, let's stay here awhile."

"You are not calm enough to stay. Come with me."

"Please, let's stay here," Troilus said. "I promise by Hell and all Hell's torments that I will not speak a word!"

"And so, good night," Diomedes said.

Cressida replied, "But you are departing in anger."

"Does that grieve you?" Troilus said. "Oh, withered truth and faithfulness!"

"How are you now?" Ulysses asked.

"By Jove, I will be calm and patient," Troilus said.

Diomedes turned to leave, and Cressida said to him, "Guardian — why, Greek!"

"Bah!" Diomedes said. "Goodbye. You are jerking me around."

"Truly, I am not," Cressida replied. "Come here once again."

Ulysses said to Troilus, "You are shaking, my lord, at something. Will you go now? You will break out in an angry fit."

Troilus said, "Cressida is stroking Diomedes' cheek!"

"Come, come," Ulysses said.

"No, let's stay," Troilus said. "By Jove, I will not speak a word. There is between my will and all offences against me a guard of calmness and patience. Stay a little while longer."

"How the Devil named Lechery, with his fat rump and potato-finger, tickles these together!" Thersites said. "Fry, lechery, fry!"

In this culture, potatoes were regarded as aphrodisiacs. The kind of tickling that Thersites was referring to is a sexual tickling, and a kind of sexual tickling was going on between Cressida and Diomedes. As for frying, the sexual tickling was heated and burning, sexual tickling can lead to the burning sensation of venereal disease, and mortals who die without sincerely repenting the sin of lechery end up burning in Hell.

"But will you, then?" Diomedes asked.

"Truly, I will," Cressida replied. "Never trust me again if I don't keep my word."

"Give me some token as a guarantee that you will keep your word," Diomedes requested.

"I'll fetch you a token," Cressida said.

She exited.

Ulysses said to Troilus, "You have sworn to be calm."

"Don't worry about me, sweet lord," Troilus said. "I will not be myself, nor will I allow myself to have knowledge of what I feel. I am all patience and nothing but calm."

Cressida returned, carrying the sleeve that Troilus had earlier given to her as a love token.

Thersites said, "Now the pledge that she will keep her word! Now! Now! Now!"

"Here, Diomedes, keep this sleeve," Cressida said as she handed him the sleeve.

"Oh, Beauty!" Troilus said. "Where is your faith? Where is your loyalty to me?"

"My lord —" Ulysses began.

"I will be calm," Troilus said. "Outwardly I will."

"Look upon that sleeve; behold it well," Cressida said, "He loved me — oh, I am a false wench! — give it back to me."

"Whose was it?" Diomedes asked.

He knew it must have belonged to Troilus, but he wanted her to say it.

"It doesn't matter, now that I have it again," Cressida said, holding the sleeve she had snatched back from Diomedes. "I will not meet with you tomorrow night. Please, Diomedes, visit me no more."

"Now she sharpens," Thersites said. "Well said, whetstone!"

Thersites thought that Cressida was playing hard to get. By doing so, she was sharpening Diomedes' desire for her.

"I shall have it," Diomedes said.

"What, this sleeve?" Cressida asked.

"Yes, that."

"Oh, all you gods!" Cressida said. "Oh, pretty, pretty pledge! Your master is now lying in his bed and thinking of you and me, and he sighs, and he takes my glove that I gave to him, and he gives it dainty kisses as he remembers me, just as I kiss the sleeve he gave to me."

Diomedes snatched the sleeve away from her.

She said, "No, do not snatch it from me. He who takes that takes my heart with it."

"I had your heart before," Diomedes said. "This follows it."

Troilus said to himself, "I swore to be calm and patient."

"You shall not have it, Diomedes; indeed, you shall not," Cressida said. "I'll give you something else."

"I will have this sleeve," Diomedes said. "Whose was it?"

"It doesn't matter."

"Come, tell me whose it was."

"It belonged to one who loved me better than you will," Cressida said. "But, now you have it, take it."

"Whose was it?" Diomedes asked again.

"By all Diana's waiting-women yonder, and by herself, I will not tell you whose."

Diana was the Moon-goddess, and her waiting women were the stars near the Moon. Diana was a virgin goddess.

Diomedes replied, "Tomorrow I will display this sleeve on my helmet, and it will grieve the spirit of a man who dares not challenge it."

Troilus said to himself, "If you were the Devil himself, and you wore it on your horn, it would be challenged."

"Well, well, it is done, it is past," Cressida said, "and yet it is not; I will not keep my word."

"Why, then, farewell," Diomedes said. "You shall never mock Diomedes again."

"You shall not go," Cressida replied. "One cannot speak a word without it immediately disturbing you."

"I do not like this fooling," Diomedes said.

Thersites said to himself, "Nor I, by Pluto, but whatever you don't like pleases me best."

"Shall I come and visit you?" Diomedes asked. "At what time?"

"Yes, come — oh, Jove! — do come — I shall be plagued," Cressida said.

"Farewell until then."

"Good night," Cressida said. "Please, come."

Diomedes exited.

"Troilus, farewell!" Cressida said to herself. "One eye still looks on you, but my other eye sees with my heart. Ah, we poor women! I find that this fault is in us: The error — the straying — of our eye directs our mind. What error leads must err. Oh, then conclude that minds swayed by eyes are full of turpitude and wickedness."

Cressida went back into her father's tent.

Thersites said to himself, "A stronger proof of what she is she could not make clearer unless she said, 'My mind is now turned whore.'"

"All's done, my lord," Ulysses said to Troilus. "There's nothing more to see."

"You are right," Troilus said.

"Why are we staying here, then?"

"To make a record in my soul of every syllable that here was spoken," Troilus replied. "But if I tell how these two carried on together, shall I not lie in publishing a truth? I still have a belief in my heart, a hope so obstinately strong that it inverts the testimony of my eyes and ears, as if those organs had deceptive functions that were created only to defame and slander. Was Cressida here?"

"I am not a magician," Ulysses replied. "I cannot conjure her spirit and make it appear, Trojan."

"Cressida was not here, I am sure."

"Most surely and definitely Cressida was here," Ulysses replied.

"Why, my negation of your assertion has no taste of madness," Troilus said.

"Nor does my assertion have a taste of madness, my lord," Ulysses said. "Cressida was here just now."

"Let it not be believed for the sake of womanhood!" Troilus said. "Remember, we had mothers; do not give advantage to stubborn critics and satirists who are apt, without a credible reason for believing in female depravity, to judge the female sex in general by Cressida's example. It is much better to think that this woman we just saw is not Cressida."

"What has she done, Prince, that can soil our mothers?" Ulysses asked.

"Nothing at all, unless this woman we saw just now were in fact Cressida," Troilus replied.

Thersites said to himself, "Will he force himself not to believe his own eyes?"

"Is this woman my Cressida?" Troilus asked. "No, this is Diomedes' Cressida. If beauty has a soul, this is not my Cressida. If souls guide vows, if vows be sanctimonious, if sanctimony be the gods' delight, if there be rule in unity itself and if one thing can be only one thing, then this is not my Cressida.

"Oh, what a mad argument — it gives reasons for and against itself! This argument has twofold authority! In it reason can revolt against itself without perdition, and madness — the loss of reason — can assume all reason without revolt. In this argument reason can contradict itself without being insane, and insanity can be rational without contradicting itself.

"The conclusion of this argument is that this woman we saw just now is, and is not, Cressida.

"Carrying on within my soul is a fight of this strange nature — a thing that is inseparable divides much wider than the sky and Earth, and yet the spacious breadth of this division admits no opening for a point through which it can enter Ariachne's broken threads."

Troilus was trying to understand the two Cressidas: the Cressida who had been attracted to him and whom he loved and the Cressida who was attracted to Diomedes and who had surrendered to Diomedes. The two Cressidas shared the same body and yet they seemed to be as far from each other as the sky is to the Earth.

The dual nature of the two Cressidas appeared in the dual nature of Ariachne, a name that combined the names of Arachne and Ariadne.

Arachne was a mortal woman who was skilled at weaving and who challenged the goddess Minerva to a weaving contest. The gods punish such mortal pride. Minerva tore the weaving that Arachne had created, and then Minerva turned Arachne into a spider.

Ariadne fell in love with Theseus, who had come to Crete to rid the island of the monstrous half-man, half-bull Minotaur, which lived in a maze and feasted on the flesh of the youths and maidens whom Athens sent each year to Crete as tribute. Ariadne gave Theseus a spool of thread that he could unwind in the maze and so find his way out after killing the Minotaur. Theseus and Ariadne left Crete together after he killed the Minotaur, but Theseus was soon unfaithful to her.

Troilus continued, "Here is an excellent piece of evidence — it is as strong as the gates that lead to the god Pluto's realm: Hell! Cressida is mine, tied with the bonds of Heaven.

"Here is another excellent piece of evidence — it is as strong as Heaven itself. The bonds of Heaven are slipped, dissolved, and loosed, and with another knot, five-finger-tied as she holds hands with Diomedes, the fractions of her faith, the tiny bits of her love, and the fragments and scraps, the bits and greasy relics of her over-eaten and finished faith — the faith that she had given to me — are now bound to Diomedes."

"Is worthy Troilus even half as seized with great emotion as he appears be?" Ulysses asked, drily.

"Yes, Greek," an upset Troilus replied, "and that shall be divulged well in symbolic wounds written in blood as red as Mars' heart when it was inflamed with sexual passion for Venus. Never has a young man loved with as eternal and as constant a soul as I have loved.

"Listen, Greek. As much as I love Cressida, by that much I hate her Diomedes. That sleeve is mine that he'll bear on his helmet. Even if the skill of the blacksmith-god Vulcan created that helmet, my sword will bite into it. Not even the dreadful hurricane-caused waterspout that sailors call the hurricano, gathered together in mass as it rises high and approaches the almighty Sun, shall dizzy with more clamor the ears of the sea-god Neptune as the waterspout falls back into the sea than shall my eager sword as it falls on Diomedes."

Thersites said to himself, "He'll tickle it for his concupy."

"Concupy" was a word combining the meanings of "concubine" and "concupiscence," or lust. Thersites meant that Troilus would rain blows on Diomedes' helmet to get revenge for taking Troilus' concubine — concupiscence, aka lust, both Troilus' and Diomedes', for Cressida would make Troilus do this.

Troilus said, "Oh, Cressida! Oh, false Cressida! False, false, false! Unfaithful, unfaithful, unfaithful! Let all untruths stand by your stained name, and they'll seem glorious by comparison."

"Oh, control yourself," Ulysses said to Troilus. "Your passionate outburst draws ears hither."

Aeneas walked over to Troilus and said, "I have been seeking you for the past hour, my lord. Hector, by this time, is arming himself in Troy. Ajax, your guard, is waiting to conduct you home."

"I'm coming, Prince," Troilus replied to Aeneas.

He then said to Ulysses, "My courteous lord, farewell."

He looked at the tent where Cressida was staying and said, "Farewell, faithless but fair woman! And, Diomedes, prepare yourself, and wear a castle on your head!"

Troilus felt that Diomedes would need strong protection for his head in this day's battle.

"I'll take you to the gates," Ulysses said.

"Accept my agitated thanks," Troilus said.

Troilus, Aeneas, and Ulysses exited.

Alone, Thersites said to himself, "I wish I could meet that rogue Diomedes! I would croak like a raven, that bird of omens; I would bode, I would bode. I would be an omen, I would prophesy.

"Patroclus will give me anything for information about this whore. A parrot will not do more for an almond than he will for a commodious drab — an accommodating whore.

"Lechery, lechery; always, there are wars and lechery; nothing else is fashionable. May a burning Devil take people who engage in wars and lechery! Let them burn with lust and combativeness and then burn with venereal disease and wounds and finally burn in Hell!"

Hector, armed and ready for battle, stood in front of the palace of his father, Priam, in Troy. With him was his wife, Andromache.

"When was my lord so much unkindly tempered that he would stop his ears against admonishment?" Andromache said. "Disarm, disarm, and do not fight today."

"You tempt me to offend you," Hector replied. "Get inside the palace. By all the everlasting gods, I'll go and fight today!"

"My dreams will, I am sure, prove to be ominous signs for this day."

"Tell me no more, I say."

As Cassandra walked over to Andromache, she asked, "Where is my brother Hector?"

"Here he is, sister-in-law," Andromache replied. "He is armed, and bloodthirsty in intent. Join with me in loud and heartfelt petition. Let's pursue him on our knees; for I have dreamed of bloody turbulence, and this whole night's dreams have been filled with the shapes and forms of slaughter."

"Oh, your dreams are true," Cassandra said.

Cassandra had the gift of prophecy — she was able to foretell the future.

"Let my trumpet sound!" Hector called to his trumpeter.

"Sound no notes of sally, for the Heavens, sweet brother," Cassandra pleaded.

A sally announced an attack.

"Be gone, I say," Hector said. "The gods have heard me swear an oath that I would do battle today."

"The gods are deaf to hot and headstrong vows," Cassandra said. "Such vows are polluted offerings to the gods; they are more abhorred than spotted livers in the sacrifice."

In a sacrifice, an animal was killed and its entrails were then examined. A spotted liver was a diseased liver — an ominous sign.

"Oh, be persuaded to stay in Troy today!" Andromache said. "Do not count it holy to hurt your loved ones by being just: it is as lawful to violently commit thefts and robberies simply so you can give lots of money to charity."

"It is the purpose that makes strong the vow; however, vows to every purpose must not hold," Cassandra said. "If one makes a vow for a bad purpose, that vow is not holy and ought not to be kept. Disarm, sweet Hector. Stay in Troy today."

"Calm yourself, I say," Hector said. "My honor keeps to the windward side of my fate — my honor takes precedence over my fated death. Every man holds life dear, but the brave man regards honor as far more precious and dearer than life."

The windward side is the favorable side.

Troilus walked over to him.

Seeing that Troilus looked very angry, Hector asked him, "How are you now, young man? Do you mean to fight today?"

Andromache said, "Cassandra, call my father-in-law, Priam, here so he can persuade Hector, my husband, to stay here in Troy today."

Cassandra left to get Priam.

Knowing that fighting while very angry can be dangerous because anger can lead one to take unnecessary risks, Hector said, "No, indeed, young Troilus; take off your armor, youth. I am today in the mood to fight chivalrously. I intend to do gallant deeds in battle today. Let your muscles grow until their knots are strong, and do not yet risk the hostile battles of the war. Disarm yourself, go, and don't doubt, brave boy, that I'll stand today for you and me and Troy."

"Brother, you have a vice of mercy in you, which better befits a lion than a man," Troilus replied.

A proverb stated, "The lion spares the suppliant."

"What vice is that, good Troilus?" Hector asked. "Criticize me for having it."

"Many times a conquered Greek falls, knocked over by the fanning wind of your fair sword, and then you bid them rise, and live."

"That is fair play," Hector replied.

"It is fool's play, by Heaven, Hector."

"What! What!"

"For the love of all the gods, let's leave the holy hermit called pity home with our mother, and when we have our armor buckled on, then let the venomous vengeance ride upon our swords. We will spur our swords to do work that will make others feel pity; we will use our reins to keep our swords away from the feeling of pity."

"No, savage, no!" Hector replied.

"Hector, this is war."

"Troilus, I don't want you to fight today."

"Who or what is able to keep me from fighting today?" Troilus said. "Not fate, not obedience, not the hand of fiery Mars beckoning me with his truncheon to retire from the fight. Not Priam and Hecuba on their knees, their eyes inflamed with the streaming of tears. Not you, my brother, with your true sword drawn, opposed to me with the intent to keep me from the battlefield, will keep me from fighting, unless you kill me."

Cassandra returned with Priam.

"Lay hold on Hector, Priam," Cassandra said. "Hold him fast. He is your crutch; if you now lose your prop and support, you who lean on Hector, and all Troy that leans on you, fall all together."

"Come, Hector, come, and go back into the palace," Priam said. "Your wife has dreamed ominous dreams; your mother has had visions; Cassandra foresees bad things happening; and I myself am like a prophet suddenly inspired to tell you that this day is ominous. Therefore, come back and go into the palace."

"Aeneas is on the battlefield, and I have promised many Greeks, and even pledged my valor, that I will appear before them on the battlefield this morning. If I don't appear on the battlefield, I will lose the valor that I have pledged."

"To pledge" is "to make a solemn promise." "A pledge" is "something given as security that a contract or a promise will be kept."

"Yes, but you shall not go," Priam said.

"I must not break my word," Hector said. "You know that I am dutiful; therefore, dear sir, let me not shame the respect I owe you, but instead give me permission to go to the battlefield with your consent and approval, which you here and now forbid me, royal Priam."

"Oh, Priam, do not yield to him!" Cassandra requested.

"Do not, dear father-in-law," Andromache said.

"Andromache, I am offended by you," Hector said. "By the love you bear me, go inside the palace."

An obedient wife, Andromache went inside the palace.

"This foolish, dreaming, superstitious girl — Cassandra — makes all these ominous prophecies," Troilus said.

"Oh, farewell, dear Hector!" Cassandra said.

Visualizing the future, she said, "Look, how you die! Look, how your eye turns pale! Look, how your wounds bleed at many openings! Listen, how Troy roars! How Hecuba cries out! How poor Andromache shrills her pain forth! Behold, distraction, frenzy, and amazement, as if they were witless buffoons, meet one another, and they all cry, 'Hector! Hector's dead! Oh, Hector!'"

"Go away! Go away!" Troilus yelled.

"Farewell — yet wait a moment!" Cassandra said. "Hector! I take my leave. You do yourself and all our Troy deceive."

Hector was the greatest Trojan warrior. If he were to die, Troy would soon fall.

Hector said to Priam, his father, "You are stunned, my liege, at her exclamations. Go in and cheer up the town. We'll go forth and fight, do deeds worthy of praise, and tell you about them this night."

"Farewell," Priam said. "May the gods stand around you and keep you safe!"

Priam went into the palace, and Hector left to go to the battlefield. Military trumpets announced action on the battlefield.

Troilus said to himself, "They are fighting, listen! Proud Diomedes, believe me, I am coming to fight you. I will lose my arm, or win my sleeve."

Carrying a letter, Pandarus walked over to Troilus.

Pandarus said, "Have you heard, my lord? Have you heard?"

"Heard what?" Troilus asked.

"Here's a letter come from yonder poor girl, Cressida," he replied.

"Let me read it."

As Troilus read the letter, Pandarus complained, "A vile cough, a vile rascally cough so troubles me, and the foolish fortune of this girl; and what with one thing, and what with another, one of these days I shall die and leave you, and I have a watery discharge from my eyes, too, and such an ache in my bones that, unless a man were cursed, I cannot tell what to think about it."

Some of his complaints, such as an ache in the bones, were symptoms of syphilis.

He then asked, "What does Cressida say in the letter there?"

"Words, words, mere words," Troilus said. "There is nothing from her heart. She intended to cause a certain result from the letter, but her letter affects me in a different way."

He tore up the letter and tossed the pieces into the air, saying, "Go, wind, to wind, there turn and change together. She continues to feed my love with words and lies, but she benefits another man with her deeds."

Alone on the battlefield, Thersites said to himself, "Now they are clapper-clawing — beating up — one another. I'll go and watch. That dissembling abominable varlet Diomedes has got that same scurvy doting foolish young Trojan knave's sleeve displayed in his helmet. I would like to see them meet so that that same young Trojan ass, who loves the whore there, might send that Greek whore-masterly and lecherous villain, who has the sleeve, back to the dissembling lecherous drab. Yes, let Troilus send Diomedes back to the lustful whore Cressida from a sleeveless — futile and fruitless — errand.

"On the other side, the Greek side, the cunning stratagem of those crafty swearing rascals, that stale old mouse-eaten dry cheese, Nestor, and that same cunning male-fox, Ulysses, has proven not to be worth a blackberry. They made a plan to set that mongrel cur, Ajax, against that dog of as bad a kind, Achilles. The result now is that the cur Ajax is prouder than the cur Achilles, and Ajax will not arm himself and fight today; whereupon the Greeks begin to proclaim and embrace ignorant barbarism, and political policy is beginning to have a bad reputation.

"Wait! Here comes the sleeve, and here comes the other one."

Diomedes backed into view, with Troilus following him.

"Don't run away," Troilus said. "Even if you were to jump into the Styx, a river in Hell, I would jump in, too, and swim after you."

"You are misinterpreting my strategic retreat," Diomedes said. "I am not fleeing from you. My concern to get an advantage in battle led me to withdraw from a place where Trojans were more numerous than Greeks. Now let's fight!"

As the two warriors fought, Thersites said to himself, "Fight for your whore, Greek! Now fight for your whore, Trojan! Now fight for the sleeve, the sleeve!"

The combat between Troilus and Diomedes carried them away from Thersites.

Hector appeared and asked Thersites, "Who are you, Greek? Are you an opponent for Hector? Do you have an honorable and noble birth? Is it appropriate for me to fight you?"

"No, no, I am a rascal," Thersites replied. "I am a scurvy railing knave. I am a very filthy rogue."

"I believe you," Hector said. "You may continue to live."

He exited to find an honorable opponent to fight.

"I thank God that you believed me," Thersites said, "but I hope that a plague will break your neck because you frightened me! What's become of the wenching rogues? I think they have swallowed one another. I would laugh at that miracle, yet it is true in a way that lechery eats itself. Lechery leads to venereal disease, which eats the body. I'll go and seek them."

Diomedes said to a servant, "Go, go, my servant, take Troilus' horse with you and present the fair steed to my lady, Cressida. Fellow, commend my service to her beauty. Tell her I have chastised the amorous Trojan, and tell her that I am her knight by proof. By defeating Troilus in battle, I have proven through combat that I, not Troilus, am her knight."

"I am going, my lord," the servant said.

He exited.

Agamemnon arrived and said to Diomedes, "Regroup! Regroup! The Trojans are overwhelming us! The fierce Polydamas has beaten down Menon. The bastard Margarelon has taken Doreus prisoner, and he stands like a colossus, waving his spear that is as huge as a beam, over the battered corpses of King Epistrophus and King Cedius. Polyxenes has been slain, Amphimachus and Thoas are mortally wounded, Patroclus has been captured or slain, and Palamedes is very hurt and bruised. The dreadful Sagittary, the Centaur who is a gifted archer, terrifies our soldiers. We must hasten, Diomedes, to reinforce the army, or we all will perish."

Nestor arrived with some soldiers who were carrying the corpse of Patroclus. He told the soldiers, "Go, carry Patroclus' body to Achilles, and tell the snail-paced Ajax to arm himself for shame. A thousand Hectors seem to be on the battlefield. Now he fights here on Galathe, his horse, and when he lacks work on horseback, soon he's there on foot, and the Greeks flee or die, like scattering schools of fish fleeing the spouting whale. Then Hector is yonder, and there the Greeks, like wisps of straw ripe for his sword's edge, fall down before him, like the mower's swath. Here, there, and everywhere, he leaves — spares — a life and then he takes a life. His dexterity so obeys his desire that he does whatever he wants to do to us, and he does so much that proof is called impossibility. Although we see his deeds on the battlefield, it is impossible to believe what we see."

Ulysses arrived and said, "Oh, have courage, have courage, Princes! Great Achilles is arming himself, weeping, cursing, and vowing vengeance. Patroclus' wounds have roused his drowsy blood, together with his mangled Myrmidons, who noseless, handless, hacked and chipped, come to him, crying against

Hector. Ajax has lost a friend and foams at the mouth, and he is armed and on the battlefield, roaring for Troilus, who has done today mad and fantastic slaughter, engaging himself in battle and getting out alive. He directs his efforts at hurting Greeks and not at being chivalric toward them like Hector, and he fights as if his lust for bloodshed, despite Greek cunning in the use of weapons, bade him conquer every Greek."

Ajax arrived and shouted, "Troilus! You coward Troilus!"

Then he exited.

Diomedes said, "Yes, there, there."

Diomedes, who also wanted to find and fight Troilus, followed Ajax.

Nestor said, "So, so, we draw together. We begin to fight together."

Achilles arrived and asked, "Where is Hector?"

He shouted, "Come, come, you boy-killer, show your face! Know what it is to meet Achilles when I am angry! Hector? Where's Hector? I will fight nobody but Hector!"

Ajax shouted, "Troilus, you coward Troilus, show your head!"

Diomedes arrived and shouted, "Troilus, I say! Where's Troilus?"

"What do you want with Troilus?" Ajax asked.

"I want to correct — punish — him by hurting him," Diomedes replied.

"If I were the general, I would give you that position before I would allow you — and not me — to hurt Troilus," Ajax said.

He shouted, "Troilus, I say! Where are you, Troilus?"

Troilus heard the shouts and showed up, saying, "Oh, traitor Diomedes! Turn your false face toward me, you traitor, and pay me your life that you owe me in return for my horse!"

To call a knight a traitor is the worst kind of insult — one that must be responded to with fighting.

"Ha, is that you there?" Diomedes asked.

"I'll fight him alone," Ajax said. "Stand aside, Diomedes."

"He is my prize," Diomedes replied. "I will not stand aside and be a spectator."

"Come, both of you lying Greeks," Troilus said. "I'll fight you both!"

They fought.

Hector arrived and said, "Troilus? Yes! Oh, well fought, my youngest brother!"

Achilles arrived and said, "Now I see you, Hector! Let's fight!"

Troilus fought Diomedes and Ajax, while Hector fought Achilles. During the fighting, the two groups became separated.

Hector had been fighting hard, and he said to Achilles, who was winded, "We can pause in our fighting, if you are willing."

"I do disdain your courtesy, proud Trojan," Achilles said. "I feel contempt for your courtesy. Be happy that my arms are out of shape. I have spent too much time in my tent and not fighting. My rest and negligence befriend you now, but you shall soon hear from me again. Until then, go and seek your fortune."

Achilles exited.

Hector said, "Fare you well. I would have held myself back and been a much fresher man had I expected to fight you."

Seeing Troilus coming toward him, he said, "How are you now, my brother!"

"Ajax has captured Aeneas!" Troilus replied. "Shall this be allowed to happen? No, by the flame — the Sun — of glorious Heaven, Ajax shall not carry him away. I'll be captured, too, or else I will rescue Aeneas! Fate, hear what I say! I don't care if I die today!"

Troilus exited.

A Greek wearing splendid armor arrived.

Hector said, "Stand, stand and fight, you Greek; you are a splendid target."

Frightened by Hector, the Greek ran away.

"No? You won't stay and fight?" Hector said. "I like your armor well; I'll smash it and tear off the rivets, but I'll be the owner of it. Won't you, beast, stay? Why, then flee; I'll hunt you for your hide."

He ran after the Greek wearing splendid armor.

Achilles said to his warriors, who were known as Myrmidons, "Come here around me, my Myrmidons. Listen carefully to what I say. Follow me while I search for Hector. Strike not a stroke against the Trojans, but keep yourselves in breath, and when I have found the bloodthirsty Hector, surround him with your weapons. In the cruelest manner, use your weapons on him. Follow me, sirs, and all my proceedings eye. It is decreed that Hector the great must die."

They exited to search for Hector.

In another part of the battlefield, Menelaus and Paris were fighting while Thersites watched and provided commentary.

Thersites said to himself, "The cuckold and the cuckold-maker — Menelaus and Paris — are at it. Now, bull! Now, dog! 'loo, Paris, 'loo! Now, my double-horned Spartan! 'loo, Paris, 'loo! The bull has the game: Beware the horns, ho!"

He was pretending that he was watching a dog bait — that is, torment — a bull in a "sport" similar to bear-baiting. Sometimes, the bear could kill a dog, but several dogs often attacked the bear all at the same time and the dogs usually won. Thersites called Menelaus a bull because he wore the horns of a cuckold. "'loo" was an abbreviated form of "Halloo" — a cry to encourage the dog. Menelaus, the King of Sparta, was a double-horned Spartan because he had the two horns of a cuckold and — in this "sport" — the two horns of a bull.

Paris and Menelaus exited while fighting, and the Trojan Margarelon showed up and said to Thersites, "Turn, slave, and fight."

"Slave" was a major insult.

Thersites asked, "Who are you?"

"A bastard son of Priam's," Margarelon replied.

"I am a bastard, too," Thersites said. "I love bastards. I am a bastard begot, bastard instructed, bastard in mind, bastard in valor. In everything I am illegitimate. One bear will not bite another bear, and so why should one bastard bite another bastard? Take heed, the quarrel's most ominous to us: If the son of a whore fights for a whore, he tempts judgment. If we fight for that whore Helen, we can end up being damned to eternity in Hell. Farewell, bastard."

Thersites walked away.

"May the Devil take you, coward!" Margarelon shouted at Thersites, who ignored him.

Margarelon left Thersites alone and went off in a different direction from the one that Thersites had taken.

Hector had killed the Greek soldier wearing the splendid armor. Now he said to the corpse, which was still wearing the armor, "Most putrefied core, so fair on the outside, your splendid armor has cost you your life. Now that my day's work is done, I'll catch my breath. Rest, sword; you have had your fill of blood and death."

He took off and put down his sword, helmet, and shield, and some pieces of his armor.

Achilles and the Myrmidons found him and surrounded him, cutting him off from his weapons and armor.

"Look, Hector, how the Sun begins to set," Achilles said. "Look at how ugly night comes breathing at the Sun's heels. With the setting and darkening of the Sun to end the day, Hector's life is ended and done."

"I am unarmed," Hector said. "Don't take this kind of advantage, Greek."

"Strike, fellows, strike," Achilles said. "This is the man I seek."

They killed Hector.

"So, Troy, you will fall next!" Achilles said. "Now, all of Troy, sink down in despair! Here lies your heart, your muscles, and your bone. On, Myrmidons, and all of you shout with all your might, 'Achilles has slain the mighty Hector.'"

Trumpets sounded. Night was falling.

"Listen!" Achilles said. "The Greek trumpets announce the end of the battle!"

More trumpets sounded.

A Myrmidon said to Achilles, "The Trojan trumpets also announce the end of the battle, my lord."

"The dragon wing of night overspreads the Earth," Achilles said, "and, as if they were obeying a tournament marshal, the armies separate. My half-supped sword, that frankly would have fed on more, is pleased with this dainty bite, and thus it goes to bed."

Achilles sheathed his sword and said, "Come, tie Hector's body to my horse's tail. Along the battlefield, I will the Trojan trail."

— 5.9 —

On another part of the battlefield stood Agamemnon, Ajax, Menelaus, Nestor, Diomedes, and others. They were marching back to the Greek camp to the sound of military drums.

Shouts sounded.

"Listen! Listen!" Agamemnon said. "What are they shouting?"

Nestor ordered, "Quiet, drums!"

The drummers stopped playing.

Soldiers shouted, "Achilles! Achilles! Hector's slain! Achilles!"

Diomedes said, "The rumor is, Hector's slain, and by Achilles."

"If that is true, Achilles ought not to brag about it," Ajax said. "Great Hector was a man as good as Achilles."

"March patiently along," Agamemnon said. "Let someone be sent to ask Achilles to see us at our tent. If the gods have befriended us and gifted us with Hector's death, great Troy is ours, and our sharp and painful wars are ended."

In another part of the battlefield, Aeneas met some Trojans.

"Stand here! We are still masters of the battlefield," Aeneas said. "Let's not return to Troy; let's stay the night here."

Troilus arrived and said, "Hector is slain."

"Hector! The gods forbid!" Aeneas said.

"He's dead," Troilus repeated, "and at the tail of the horse belonging to his murderer, he is being dragged as if he were a beast through the shameful battlefield. Frown on, you Heavens, effect your rage at Troy with speed! Sit, gods, upon your thrones, and smile at Troy! I say, at once let loose your plagues on us. If your plagues kill us quickly, you will show us mercy. We are sure to be destroyed, so we pray that you don't destroy us slowly — instead, destroy us quickly!"

"My lord, you are discouraging all the soldiers!" Aeneas said.

"You misunderstand me when you tell me that," Troilus replied. "I am not talking about flight, fear, and death; instead, I dare to face all approaching perils that gods and men can direct against us. Hector is dead and gone. Who shall tell Priam that, or tell Hecuba? Let him who will tell them be forever called a screech owl — a bird of bad omens. Go into Troy, and say there, 'Hector's dead.' Those words will turn Priam to stone. They will make wells and Niobes of the maidens and wives; their eyes will well with tears, and the mothers will grieve like Niobe when her seven sons and seven daughters all died on the same day. They will make cold statues of the youths, and they will scare Troy out of itself. But, march away to Troy. Hector is dead; there is no more to say.

"But wait a moment."

He looked at the Greek camp and said, "You vile abominable Greek tents, thus proudly set up on our Trojan plains, let Titan — the Sun — rise as early as he dares, I'll charge through you and through you! And, you great-sized coward, Achilles, no space of earth shall separate our two hatreds of each other. I'll constantly haunt you like a wicked conscience that creates goblins as swiftly as the thoughts of madness."

He then said to his fellow Trojans, "Have the drums strike a quick march to Troy! March back to Troy, and take with you this comforting thought: Hope of revenge shall hide our inward woe."

Aeneas, the drummers, and the other Trojans marched away.

Pandarus walked over to Troilus and said, "Listen! Listen!"

Bitterly, Troilus said to Pandarus, "Go away, broker-lackey — go-between and hanger-on! May ignominy and shame pursue you throughout your life, and may they always be associated with your name!"

Troilus left.

Alone, Pandarus said bitterly to himself, "Troilus' words are a 'splendid medicine' for my aching bones! Oh, world! World! World! Thus is the poor agent despised! Oh, traitors and bawds, how earnestly are you set to work, and how ill is your work rewarded! Why should our endeavor be so loved and the performance so loathed? What verse can express this? What example can I use? Let me see."

He sang this song:

"Full merrily the bumblebee does sing,

"Until he has lost his honey and his sting;

"And being once subdued in armed tail,

"Sweet honey and sweet notes together fail."

A bumblebee — that is, a man — can be happy and sing as long as his sting — his erect penis — can produce honey — semen. But when his tail — penis — no longer can get erect, then he can produce no honey and stops singing.

Pandarus then looked you readers of this book directly in the eyes and said, "Good traders in the flesh, write that song in your painted cloths."

A painted cloth is a cheap substitute for a tapestry. Often, a painted cloth contains a moral of some kind.

Pandarus continued, "As many as be here in the pander's hall — the place where you are reading this book — your eyes, half blind, should weep at Pandarus' fall. But if you cannot weep, yet give some groans, though if you do not groan for me, you can still groan for your own aching bones."

Aching bones are a symptom of syphilis.

"Brethren and sisters of the hold-door trade — my fellow bawds and panders who watch the door while fornicators are in the room — approximately two months from now my will shall here be revealed. That is when I expect to die. My will should be read out loud and you should receive your bequests now, but my fear is this: Some galled goose — syphilitic whore — of the nearby brothel district would hiss. Let it be known that a hiss is an inappropriate critical response to this book. Until I die I'll sweat as a treatment for my venereal diseases and seek about for ways to ease the pain. For now I seek good eases, but when I die I bequeath to you my diseases."

Appendix A: About the Author

It was a dark and stormy night. Suddenly a cry rang out, and on a hot summer night in 1954, Josephine, wife of Carl Bruce, gave birth to a boy — me. Unfortunately, this young married couple allowed Reuben Saturday, Josephine's brother, to name their first-born. Reuben, aka "The Joker," decided that Bruce was a nice name, so he decided to name me Bruce Bruce. I have gone by my middle name — David — ever since.

Being named Bruce David Bruce hasn't been all bad. Bank tellers remember me very quickly, so I don't often have to show an ID. It can be fun in charades, also. When I was a counselor as a teenager at Camp Echoing Hills in Warsaw, Ohio, a fellow counselor gave the signs for "sounds like" and "two words," then she pointed to a bruise on her leg twice. Bruise Bruise? Oh yeah, Bruce Bruce is the answer!

Uncle Reuben, by the way, gave me a haircut when I was in kindergarten. He cut my hair short and shaved a small bald spot on the back of my head. My mother wouldn't let me go to school until the bald spot grew out again.

Of all my brothers and sisters (six in all), I am the only transplant to Athens, Ohio. I was born in Newark, Ohio, and have lived all around Southeastern Ohio. However, I moved to Athens to go to Ohio University and have never left.

At Ohio U, I never could make up my mind whether to major in English or Philosophy, so I got a bachelor's degree with a double major in both areas, then I added a Master of Arts degree in English and a Master of Arts degree in Philosophy. Yes, I have my MAMA degree.

Currently, and for a long time to come (I eat fruits and veggies), I am spending my retirement writing books such as *Nadia Comaneci: Perfect 10*, *The Funniest People in Dance*, *Homer's* Iliad: *A Retelling in Prose*, and *William Shakespeare's* Othello: *A Retelling in Prose*.

By the way, my sister Brenda Kennedy writes romances such as *A New Beginning* and *Shattered Dreams*.

Appendix B: Some Books by David Bruce

Retellings of a Classic Work of Literature

Arden of Faversham*: A Retelling*

Ben Jonson's The Alchemist: *A Retelling*

Ben Jonson's The Arraignment, or Poetaster: *A Retelling*

Ben Jonson's Bartholomew Fair: *A Retelling*

Ben Jonson's The Case is Altered: *A Retelling*

Ben Jonson's Catiline's Conspiracy: *A Retelling*

Ben Jonson's The Devil is an Ass: *A Retelling*

Ben Jonson's Epicene: *A Retelling*

Ben Jonson's Every Man in His Humor: *A Retelling*

Ben Jonson's Every Man Out of His Humor: *A Retelling*

Ben Jonson's The Fountain of Self-Love, or Cynthia's Revels: *A Retelling*

Ben Jonson's The Magnetic Lady, or Humors Reconciled: *A Retelling*

Ben Jonson's The New Inn, or The Light Heart: *A Retelling*

Ben Jonson's Sejanus' Fall: *A Retelling*

Ben Jonson's The Staple of News: *A Retelling*

Ben Jonson's A Tale of a Tub: *A Retelling*

Ben Jonson's Volpone, or the Fox: *A Retelling*

Christopher Marlowe's Complete Plays: Retellings

Christopher Marlowe's Dido, Queen of Carthage: *A Retelling*

Christopher Marlowe's Doctor Faustus: *Retellings of the 1604 A-Text and of the 1616 B-Text*

Christopher Marlowe's Edward II: *A Retelling*

Christopher Marlowe's The Massacre at Paris: *A Retelling*

Christopher Marlowe's The Rich Jew of Malta: *A Retelling*

Christopher Marlowe's Tamburlaine, Parts 1 and 2: *Retellings*

Dante's Divine Comedy: *A Retelling in Prose*

Dante's Inferno: *A Retelling in Prose*

Dante's Purgatory: *A Retelling in Prose*

Dante's Paradise: *A Retelling in Prose*

The Famous Victories of Henry V: *A Retelling*

From the Iliad *to the* Odyssey: *A Retelling in Prose of Quintus of Smyrna's* Posthomerica

George Chapman, Ben Jonson, and John Marston's Eastward Ho! *A Retelling*

George Peele's The Arraignment of Paris: *A Retelling*

George Peele's The Battle of Alcazar: *A Retelling*

George's Peele's David and Bathsheba, and the Tragedy of Absalom: *A Retelling*

George Peele's Edward I: *A Retelling*

George Peele's The Old Wives' Tale: *A Retelling*

George-a-Greene: *A Retelling*

The History of King Leir: *A Retelling*
Homer's Iliad: *A Retelling in Prose*
Homer's Odyssey: *A Retelling in Prose*
J.W. Gent.'s The Valiant Scot: *A Retelling*
Jason and the Argonauts: A Retelling in Prose of Apollonius of Rhodes' Argonautica
John Ford: Eight Plays Translated into Modern English
John Ford's The Broken Heart: *A Retelling*
John Ford's The Fancies, Chaste and Noble: *A Retelling*
John Ford's The Lady's Trial: *A Retelling*
John Ford's The Lover's Melancholy: *A Retelling*
John Ford's Love's Sacrifice: *A Retelling*
John Ford's Perkin Warbeck: *A Retelling*
John Ford's The Queen: *A Retelling*
John Ford's 'Tis Pity She's a Whore: *A Retelling*
John Lyly's Campaspe: *A Retelling*
John Lyly's Endymion, The Man in the Moon: *A Retelling*
John Lyly's Galatea: *A Retelling*
John Lyly's Love's Metamorphosis: *A Retelling*
John Lyly's Midas: *A Retelling*
John Lyly's Mother Bombie: *A Retelling*
John Lyly's Sappho and Phao: *A Retelling*
John Lyly's The Woman in the Moon: *A Retelling*
John Webster's The White Devil: *A Retelling*
King Edward III: *A Retelling*
Mankind: *A Medieval Morality Play* (A Retelling)
Margaret Cavendish's The Unnatural Tragedy: *A Retelling*
The Merry Devil of Edmonton: *A Retelling*
The Summoning of Everyman: *A Medieval Morality Play* (A Retelling)
Robert Greene's Friar Bacon and Friar Bungay: *A Retelling*
The Taming of a Shrew: *A Retelling*
Tarlton's Jests: A Retelling
Thomas Middleton's A Chaste Maid in Cheapside: *A Retelling*
Thomas Middleton's Women Beware Women: *A Retelling*
Thomas Middleton and Thomas Dekker's The Roaring Girl: *A Retelling*
Thomas Middleton and William Rowley's The Changeling: *A Retelling*
The Trojan War and Its Aftermath: Four Ancient Epic Poems
Virgil's Aeneid: *A Retelling in Prose*
William Shakespeare's 5 Late Romances: Retellings in Prose
William Shakespeare's 10 Histories: Retellings in Prose
William Shakespeare's 11 Tragedies: Retellings in Prose
William Shakespeare's 12 Comedies: Retellings in Prose
William Shakespeare's 38 Plays: Retellings in Prose

William Shakespeare's 1 Henry IV, aka Henry IV, Part 1: *A Retelling in Prose*

William Shakespeare's 2 Henry IV, aka Henry IV, Part 2: *A Retelling in Prose*

William Shakespeare's 1 Henry VI, aka Henry VI, Part 1: *A Retelling in Prose*

William Shakespeare's 2 Henry VI, aka Henry VI, Part 2: *A Retelling in Prose*

William Shakespeare's 3 Henry VI, aka Henry VI, Part 3: *A Retelling in Prose*

William Shakespeare's All's Well that Ends Well: *A Retelling in Prose*

William Shakespeare's Antony and Cleopatra: *A Retelling in Prose*

William Shakespeare's As You Like It: *A Retelling in Prose*

William Shakespeare's The Comedy of Errors: *A Retelling in Prose*

William Shakespeare's Coriolanus: *A Retelling in Prose*

William Shakespeare's Cymbeline: *A Retelling in Prose*

William Shakespeare's Hamlet: *A Retelling in Prose*

William Shakespeare's Henry V: *A Retelling in Prose*

William Shakespeare's Henry VIII: *A Retelling in Prose*

William Shakespeare's Julius Caesar: *A Retelling in Prose*

William Shakespeare's King John: *A Retelling in Prose*

William Shakespeare's King Lear: *A Retelling in Prose*

William Shakespeare's Love's Labor's Lost: *A Retelling in Prose*

William Shakespeare's Macbeth: *A Retelling in Prose*

William Shakespeare's Measure for Measure: *A Retelling in Prose*

William Shakespeare's The Merchant of Venice: *A Retelling in Prose*

William Shakespeare's The Merry Wives of Windsor: *A Retelling in Prose*

William Shakespeare's A Midsummer Night's Dream: *A Retelling in Prose*

William Shakespeare's Much Ado About Nothing: *A Retelling in Prose*

William Shakespeare's Othello: *A Retelling in Prose*

William Shakespeare's Pericles, Prince of Tyre: *A Retelling in Prose*

William Shakespeare's Richard II: *A Retelling in Prose*

William Shakespeare's Richard III: *A Retelling in Prose*

William Shakespeare's Romeo and Juliet: *A Retelling in Prose*

William Shakespeare's The Taming of the Shrew: *A Retelling in Prose*

William Shakespeare's The Tempest: *A Retelling in Prose*

William Shakespeare's Timon of Athens: *A Retelling in Prose*

William Shakespeare's Titus Andronicus: *A Retelling in Prose*

William Shakespeare's Troilus and Cressida: *A Retelling in Prose*

William Shakespeare's Twelfth Night: *A Retelling in Prose*

William Shakespeare's The Two Gentlemen of Verona: *A Retelling in Prose*

William Shakespeare's The Two Noble Kinsmen: *A Retelling in Prose*

William Shakespeare's The Winter's Tale: *A Retelling in Prose*